CHILDREN OF PLAINS

ESTATES

I0536543

SILENT TEARS

B

By

Claudette Milner

Claudette Milner

Dedication

This book is dedicated to my mother, Hazel Milner

August 2, 1934 – August 7, 2011,
May She Rest in Peace

Claudette Milner

Acknowledgments

First, to God be the Glory for I write only by his grace. Thank my family and friends for your support, love, and prayers.

Table of Contents

Prologue

Allen Bates had been betrayed by a father who molested him, a system that betrayed him, and a school that looked the other way when he was bullied. Instead of compassion, the church passed judgment on his mother after she divorced the man who abused her child.

A Priest molested Alfredo Hernandez. His father settled out of court, moved, and began a new life where his son's secret remained with his family.

Alfredo struggled to keep his faith. His fight was with God whom he felt betrayed him.

For Glen, there was no refuge. His father was free, His classmates taunted him. He was treated as a criminal instead of a victim. After killing his father he could not find peace. As his peers bullied him he took away the pain himself with a bullet to his head in front of his persecutors.

CHAPTER 1

Dr. Smith was rounding the corner when he heard the gunshot. He saw Alan's small, slim body collapse against the cold linoleum tile. Justin felt wet as urine trickled down his leg. His body had betrayed him. He had peed on himself. Carl screamed repeatedly

"Oh my God, Oh my God! We didn't mean it! We didn't mean it!"

Dr. Smith checked on Alan. He cradled him in his arms. There was nothing that could be done. He had a single shot to the brain. The shot was meant to kill and not to maim. He held him in his arms oblivious to the blood stains on his shirt. Instinctively he knew he had to move to help the other two boys. One was in shock and the other was trembling. He laid Alan's body down, covered it with his jacket, and went to examine the other two boys.

The principal ran down the hallway when he heard the shot. He stopped short when he saw the scene and called the police.

Dr. Smith yelled. "Get some blankets and the school nurse. I dropped my bag at the front entrance. Please bring it to me."

The principal seemed frozen in his tracks, then he began to move. He radioed for the nurse and the blankets. They all heard the ambulances wailing in the background. He said a silent prayer.

7

"Dear God, help us through this."
The police immediately locked the classroom down. Glen knew that it had something to do with Alan. He was filled with hope. Maybe they found Alan. He knew that he would be arrested. He had committed a crime but so had his dad and he was given a second chance. Alan needed help. He needed someone to understand his pain, his torture. Night after night he woke up with nightmares of his father's abuse. His life would never be the same. Where was his justice? Glen sat on the floor with his legs crossed, his head in her hands as instructed. He thought about the good times he had shared with Alan instead of the reality he knew would come.

Ellen heard the phone ring. She picked it up quickly, not wanting to wake Mrs. Bates until necessary. She hadn't slept all night. When she heard the news she trembled. "Mrs. Smith," asked the officer.

"Are you still there?"

"Yes, I'm here,"

he heard Ellen say faintly so low he could barely hear her voice.

"We are sending a car to take Mrs. Bates to the school," replied the officer.

Ellen thought. *How do you prepare a mother for the news of the death of her son? Her son had killed her husband and now her son was dead. How does one survive such a tragedy?"*

Ellen checked on Elizabeth and went in to wake Janice. Janice
sat up when she entered the room.

"I heard the telephone ring. Did they find Alan?" she asked
anxiously.

She knew they had a long road ahead of them but all she could think
about was that she would have her son with her. They would go from
there regardless of the outcome.

Ellen braced herself to tell Janice the news. Ellen took Janice's
hands in hers. As she delivered the news, she squeezed her hands
tighter. Janice's body collapsed against hers. Her sobs exploded.
Ellen heard the police car pull up. She had to keep Elizabeth. She
could not be there with Janice. A lady detective accompanied Mrs.
Bates to the school. The ride seemed like an eternity. Ellen woke
Elizabeth. She needed to be at the school to speak with her son. What
would she say to him? She shuttered and then began to move. She
had to be with her husband and her son.

"We need to get the boys to the hospital," said Dr. Smith.
"We have grief counselors on the way," said the officer.

"Dr . Smith, Mrs. Bates is on the way. We have a female
officer with her. Dr. Smith, do you have any idea what
happened?"

"The boys will need to be questioned?" replied Dr. Smith.
"We know that there was an incident between them, and it
resulted in the suicide of Alan Bates."

"That's all we know right now," said the officer.

"The boys' parents will be meeting us at the hospital. We want to handle this by the book. We will also need to talk to your son when he's ready about the incident in the school cafeteria yesterday." "They are bringing Glen to the office so I can speak with him," replied Dr. Smith.

They both looked up when they heard Mrs. Bates sob.

She ran to her son's body, kneeling beside him and then taking him into her arms. "Why God have you taken my son from me?" cried Mrs. Bates. "Why did you take him? I am responsible for all of this. It is my fault. I should have killed him myself. I shouldn't have left it for my son to do what needed to be done. I should have killed him when he first violated my son. I should have been the one to kill him."

Dr. Smith kneeled beside Mrs. Bates

"Janice, this is not your fault. Our system failed Alan. You have Elizabeth to rear now. You have to go on for her."

Janice stood up. "I cannot go on until I get justice for my son. There must be justice for my son."

Ellen came in the back way. Mrs. Bates and Glen were in the office waiting for her. Ellen's immediate concern was for her son. Mrs. Bates took Elizabeth while Ellen went to her son. Glen had been taken to a separate room. Just as Ellen was about to enter the room, Dr. Smith walked into the office. Ellen looked at him. She gasped when she saw the blood. He looked down. He had removed the shirt but still had on the t-shirt. The office assistant offered him a school sweatshirt.

"Go on in Ellen," said Dr. Smith. "I will join you as soon as I change into this shirt." Ellen wanted to embrace her husband, but she knew her son needed her more. Glen ran to his mom as soon as she walked into the door.

"Mom, it's bad isn't it?" cried Glen. "I heard the ambulance. Did they take Alan to the hospital? He's all right, isn't he? He's just hurt right?" Glen was almost yelling.

Just then Dr. Smith came into the room.

"Dr. Smith did you go to the hospital with Alan?" questioned Glen. "When can I see him? Can we go to the hospital now?" Ellen gathered her son in her arms.

"Glen, Alan is dead. He committed suicide," said his mom. "The pain was just too much for him. He didn't want to live anymore." Glen's body seemed to crumble in her arms. Dr. Smith came over to comfort his wife and his son.

"Ellen," said Dr. Smith.

"Janice is waiting for you. There are news cameras and reporters out front. Take both of them out the back."

"No, they both looked to the door where they saw Janice Bates.

"Ellen, you, and Tom have been wonderful, but I   will speak with the press. I have to do this for my son."

"Janice, do you want me to go with you?" asked Ellen.

"I would appreciate it if you would stay here with Elizabeth," replied Janice. "Then we can leave."

"We will be here waiting for you," said Dr. Smith.

Janice went to the front door to face the press. There was quiet as she began to speak.

 "I will make a statement, but I will not answer any questions." Janice began to speak.

"My son killed himself today because the pain of living was too much to bear. My son was molested by his father. The justice system plea bargained his case. His accuser was in rehabilitation after six months... Where were you when they plea-bargained this case? Where were you when the children taunted my son calling him names even though he was the victim. Where was my church when my husband was released? They were sitting in the pulpit gossiping and passing judgment on my family. Now, you are here. My husband is dead. My son is dead. Now we are newsworthy. Why did it take a tragedy to happen for you to report his story?"

Janice began to cry, tears streaming down her face. Ellen Smith walked out to the front of the school and hugged her friend, thinking of how courageous this woman was and how dedicated she was to turning her son's tragedy into a victory for survivors of sexual abuse.

When Pastor Simms heard what had happened he closed himself off into his parish to pray.

"God, I have failed your daughter. I do not know how to make it right. Lead me in your ways."

Pastor Simms knew what he must do. He drove to the school. All the press would be gone so he would not be using her grief for the sake of his guilt. He walked through the thinning crowd. He reached out to Sister Bates and said

"I am so sorry. I have failed you. He turned to the crowd. God has not failed this wonderful child of God but we the church and the community have failed her. Please join me in praying for her family and the restoration of the church. Please take each other's hand regardless of denomination. Let us pray. "Father God......

As they prayed, one station was still filming. In the background behind the center of events was an independent reporter determined to tell this young man's story. That night this story would be played throughout the world. Its impact would never be known.

Janice took her daughter in her arms. "I would like to go home with my daughter and remember the good times with my son."

A smile came across her face as she thought about the day they laid her beautiful son in her arms, perfect and innocent. They all walked to the car in silence. This day would be forever engrained in their memory.

Ellen turned to her husband. She knew Glen still had to be questioned.

"Tomorrow," said Dr. Smith.

"Everything else can wait until tomorrow."
Ellen nodded in agreement.

Mr. Hernandez and his wife were watching the news when Alan Bates' story came on the television. Mr. Hernandez quickly gathered his children. They took each other's hand and began to pray. It didn't matter that the news went directly to another clip they continued to pray for Alan and all the other victims. Mr. Hernandez thought *"Only by the grace of God is this not my son. Please God let no other child be harmed."*

Mr. Hernandez would reach out to this brave woman and her family for he knew her pain.

"Dad," said Alfredo. "I would like to go to the service. May I go?"

"Yes Alfredo," we will get the information from the paper. We all will go he said with tears in his eyes. He hugged his son. He held on to his son for what seemed like forever. He looked at his son and his daughter Adriana. I love you very much. His children went upstairs. Mrs. Hernandez hugged her husband and cried, knowing this could have been their family.

CHAPTER 2

The small church was filled with people. Some members came to the service, but most had never met Mrs. Bates or her son. Children from the school came to say goodbye. Most of them had never befriended Alan but, they had felt the pain of being isolated from the various clicks.. They, more than others, understood his pain Somehow they hoped that this incident would make their lives easier. They silently wondered if the teasing and heckling would stop after Alan's death. Most remained cynical. The school had set up group sessions to discuss the problem, but it was a ruse, fake. The bullies claimed to gain understanding and the victims didn't speak out for fear of retaliation. Didn't grown-ups understand anything? Justin and Carl now understood the consequences of their actions. The memory of Alan Bates shooting himself in the head would always be with them, but would they make others understand what they had now experienced? They were their only hope to bridge the gap between the perpetrators and the victims.

The service was short. Mrs. Bates wanted it that way.

After the service, Mr. Hernandez and Alfredo went to speak with Mrs. Bates.

"Mrs. Bates," spoke Alfredo cautiously.

"My name is Alfredo Hernandez; This is my father. I wanted to be here because I am a survivor of sexual abuse. I want to thank you for your courage in telling your story. I did not know your son, but I do know his pain because I have lived it. I am so sorry for your loss."

Mrs. Bates knelt and hugged this small boy and then hugged Mr. Hernandez.

"Thank you for coming. It means so much to me." She looked at Alfredo and said,

"thank you for having the courage to share your story with me. You are a brave boy." Your parents must be enormously proud to have raised such a wonderful son.

Ellen and Dr. Smith took Mrs. Bates home. Mr. Bates' family had not attended the funeral. They had a separate service for their son. They wasted no time in filing for custody of Elizabeth, claiming that Janice had been an unfit parent. The state was talking about pressing charges against Justin and Carl implicating them in Alan's death. It was not enough that Janice had lost her son now she had to go through a custody hearing and possibly a trial. Her son had more rights dead, than he did while alive. How ironic was that? Ellen was going home to spend time with her son and then she would stay the night with Janice. She knew what a difficult night this would be for her. When Ellen and Tom pulled up in the driveway they saw a familiar car. A door opened and Derrick exited his car and walked toward them. Ellen nodded to Glen before he had a chance to ask. Ellen understood how devastating Alan's death had been for her son. He needed the support of all his family.

She was so happy Derrick had come to be with him. She saw
Derrick hug his son and then he walked over to Ellen and Tom.
Derrick spoke first.

"I didn't mean to intrude, and I know this is not my weekend, but
I wanted my son to know that I am here for him."

"Derrick, I'm glad you came," replied Ellen. "Glen needs you
right now. Glen, it is okay if you would like to spend some time
with your father. We understand."

"Dad, do you have time?" asked Glen. "Just your coming is
enough."

"Glen, I cleared my schedule just in case you needed to talk or
just wanted to share some things with me about you and Alan's
friendship," explained Derrick.

This was a new role for Derrick. He didn't know what to say or
how to act. He just wanted to be there for his son. Derrick
looked at Tom and Ellen for help. Tom stepped in. He wanted to
make Derrick comfortable for Glen's sake.

"Derrick, why don't you and Glen get a bite to eat and just be
there for him? You will know what he needs. The most
important thing you could have done was to be here. Everything
else will fall into place."

Glen hugged his parents. "I love you both. Thank you for

understanding."

Derrick drove Glen to their favorite spot to eat and then drove to his garage where they could share some private time. This had become their refuge. This was the place they had begun to get

to know each other again. Here they had laughed, and they had cried. They sat on the couch and Glen began to talk with tears streaming down his eyes. "Alan was one of my first real friends. He was in the slow class with me. We bonded because we both had skipped school and had problems at home. When Alan told me about his father I promised to keep his secret, but he got sick. I had to get Dr. Smith to help him. That's when his father was arrested, and he left school for a while. When he came back to school, I wasn't in the slow class. I had new friends. I didn't know what to say to him, so I stayed away like the other kids. I wasn't there for him like I should have been. Maybe if I had been a better friend this wouldn't have happened. Alan told me he was having nightmares when he found out his dad was going to be released. He told me how people who knew the truth in his neighborhood had teased him when they found out. I knew how bad things were for him. I should have done something. When Dr. Smith agreed to help his mom pay for a tutor and she started the catering business Alan seemed happier. How could I have missed the signs? Why did they let his father out of jail? They were beginning to rebuild their family. Who put it on the internet? How did Carl and Justin find out? How could anyone be so cruel? How can anyone be so cruel?"

Derrick just let his son cry. He had no answers. All he could do was hold him.

Carl woke up screaming in the middle of the night. His mother was sitting at his bedside. Every time he would drift off

to sleep he would see Alan Bates put the gun to his head and shoot himself. He would see all the blood. He remembered the man cradling his body then closing his eyes and laying a jacket over the body. Then he was led away to the office, and someone kept asking him question after question until he couldn't stop screaming. Then he felt a needle prick his arm. First, there was pain then it was gone. He could no longer hear the questions.

Mrs. Blevins got up and changed her son's pajamas and sheets. He had wet the bed. She had given her son a sedative to make him sleep. She mourned for Alan Bates and his family, but no amount of pain could bring him back to life. What would happen to her son? He had been released in her custody until after a psychiatric evaluation. What price would he have to pay for his actions?

Justin's parents were in denial. Justin was raised in a Christian home. He would never treat someone so cruelly. The principal's office had called that morning and said the boys were being suspended but they thought it was just a juvenile prank. After all, boys will be boys, Sometimes things get out of hand. The other boy had probably provoked their son to say such cruel things. What their son had been taught was that what happened between that boy and his father was a sin and that they were going to hell. He probably was trying to help the boy. The fact that they could file criminal charges against her son for

accessory to a crime was outrageous. How could they blame their son for telling the truth? The father and the son were sinners. They both paid for their sins and now they want to blame my son. Mr. Houston hired an attorney to represent their son. Justin did not want an attorney. He could not tell his parents it was he who looked up the website and made the comment to Alan in front of everyone in the cafeteria. It was his fault that Alan Bates was dead. Carl just went along because he wanted to fit in. Justin did try to convince his parents to hire an attorney for Carl. Carl's mother can't afford one. He would have to use a state-appointed attorney.

Justin had heard people talking in the hallway. There were too many of these school killings. It was time that a precedent was set in cases like these. He was scared. He didn't know what to do. Did he shift the blame to save himself? Carl wasn't even rational. The only thing he knew was that he was going to have a psychiatric evaluation. His attorney was going to use it to their benefit. His parents had advised him to not say a word and do whatever the attorney advised him. For now, he would keep quiet.

Janice heard a knock on the door and was sure it was Ellen. She was surprised when she looked out and it was Mrs. Ware. She wanted to turn the lights off and walk the other way, but she answered the door. Janice held the door open and said quietly under her breath

"Come in Agnes"

"Thank you for letting me in Janice. I realize I am the last person you expected to see. I am one of the church members that talked about your husband. I told myself I was protecting the other members, but I was gossiping. My actions contributed to your pain and for that, I am deeply sorry. I can't speak for anyone but myself, but I am ashamed of the way I treated you. I hope eventually you will find it in your heart to forgive me."
Janice hugged her.
"I forgive you because you are sincere. Thank you so much for coming."
"I would like to sit with you for a while if you will let me. I can cook something for you and Elizabeth or bath her if you want me to," inquired Agnes.

"Agnes, I would love it if you would talk with me. Elizabeth is sleeping. The quiet is as loud as thunder. It fills the house with visions of my son, his laughter, his tears, his drums pounding, his symbols crashing, and it is overwhelming. Please talk to me to quiet the sounds."

"Alfredo, I am so proud of you," said Adriana. "I never really understood how much pain you were in until now. When I read Alan Bates's story, I learned more about how courageous you are. I want you to know that I love you. I know you are still in counseling, but I am your sister. If you need to talk I am here for you. I know I said that before. When you tried to talk with

me I judged you. This time I am just here to listen." Alfredo hugged his sister. They had reached a new level of understanding.

CHAPTER 3

Toni sat down on the couch. She was tired and drained. She had a hectic schedule between completing her counseling internship and caring for the family. She had cut down to two AA meetings a month unless she felt she needed an additional session. Bill had finally started attending Al-Anon meetings. Everything was finally on track. The children had finally begun to trust her. She decided to take a shower before dinner, so she hurried upstairs. She had about 45 minutes before solitude became chaos. Betsy was off today. Thursdays were special for her. She missed being in charge of her kitchen. She knew Betsy had been the one taking care of the household while she was in rehabilitation, and she would always be grateful but sometimes she was jealous of her relationship with the children. She ran the cold water on high. It stung at first then it was soothing. Once a month she checked her breast to make sure there were no abnormalities. Her mother had died of breast cancer, and she knew that early detection was important. She examined her left breast. She smiled at first then got more serious when she felt a very slight lump on the right breast. She checked the left breast again, then checked the right. She would let her doctor know about the lump during her next check-up. Every voice in her head screamed don't wait go now! It is probably nothing. I'll call Mary Humpries and see what she thinks tonight after the children go to bed. Toni heard the children come in the door and call her name. She had let the time slip away from her. She called downstairs and said she would be down in a few minutes. She dressed in a pair of jeans and then quickly changed. The children were used to her being dressed for class on Thursdays. She put on some slacks and a blouse, brushed her hair, and went downstairs. She thought *everything would be ok.* She was afraid but she couldn't worry the children. They had been through enough.

"Mom," asked Tammy.

"When will dinner be ready? I know you have your class tonight.

"Maybe we should go out to dinner tonight to give Mom a break." chided Tommy.

"Right, you mean give yourselves a break from my cooking," joked Mrs. Colbert.

The phone rang. Mrs. Colbert picked it up. It was Bill.

"Hon, I am running late," said Mr. Colbert.

'Is it too late for you and the kids to meet me at Tommy's job?" We could grab some burgers and give him a ride home. You haven't cooked have you?"

"I am beginning to believe this is a conspiracy because nobody is surprised you called," replied Mrs. Colbert.

"I confess," said Bill jokingly. "You have been looking a little tired lately. I thought maybe you could use a break."

"I did need to speak with Mary about my internship so we can go to dinner and then stop at her house. I'll give her a call and

see if she's busy tonight. What time are you going to be ready?" asked Toni.

"Why don't you meet me at the restaurant at 6:00 p.m.?" queried Bill.

"Okay Bill, we'll meet you there."

Toni decided to call Mary before she left for the restaurant and see if John needed a ride home from work. Toni picked up the telephone to call. The telephone rang several times. She felt relieved when Mary answered the phone.

"Hello, Mary.

"It's Toni Colbert. I was hoping I could stop by later and talk with you. It's pretty important. We are going to the boys' job to eat, and I thought maybe I could bring John home and discuss my internship with you," asked Toni.

Mary could tell by the tone in Toni's voice that this had nothing to do with her internship. She also knew she was censoring what she said.

"Toni, I look forward to seeing you," said Mary. Thanks for picking John up from work."

"Thanks, Mary. I would appreciate it if you would keep this between you and me."

Toni was unusually quiet during dinner. She tried hard to listen

25

and participate in the conversation laughing at all the right times.

Bill wasn't fooled in the least. Toni had looked

tired lately. He knew she had a busy schedule, but this was

different. He had been through her drinking spells enough to
know that she was not back on the bottle. He knew she was
probably going to Mary's to discuss it with her. He was trying
hard not to let it get to him, but he thought she trusted him. They
had been in counseling for over a year now. They were working
on rebuilding their trust. He thought that Toni and he could
discuss anything. In his more rational state, he knew that she
needed some time and would come to him in her own time but in
his heart, he felt it was rejection.

"Toni, I'm going to take Debbie and Tommy home with me. Tell
Mary and Henry I said hello and we will talk soon," said Bill.
Toni kissed her husband.

"Thank you for understanding. I'll tell you everything tonight. I
promise."

Bill kissed her back. He immediately regretted his thoughts. He
was working hard at silencing his demons, but he still had a way
to go.

Toni pulled the car into the driveway. She hesitated for a minute
then turned and spoke with the boys.

"Tommy, I need to speak with Mary for a few minutes. You

can visit with John while I talk with her," said Mrs. Colbert.

Toni saw the concern on her son's face. He had noticed that his

mom always looked tired lately. He wondered if she was sick.

They were used to her being drunk, but she had never been sick.

"Tommy, everything is fine. I need to talk with Mary about my

practicum."

Mary and Toni went to the den where they could talk in private.

"Toni, sit down and tell me what's wrong. Is it work or

something more personal?"

Toni's voice trembled as she spoke. "I was taking a shower today

and I felt a lump under my left armpit. My mother died of breast

cancer, and I guess it has me shaken. I am just getting my life

back after so many years. I can't be dying. Is this my punishment

for what I put my family through living with an alcoholic?"

Toni let the tears come. She had been afraid when she first

began feeling tired of completing the simplest tasks. She ignored

it until she felt the lump. Mary held her hand and let her cry. She

was a nurse. She knew that finding a lump was immediately

associated with cancer and a death sentence. This was different

for her. She wasn't a nurse giving encouraging information. This

was someone who had become a close friend. She knew she had

to put her emotions aside and give Toni the information that she

needed to know.

"Toni, I know this is scary but finding a lump doesn't

immediately mean you have cancer; however you do need to see a doctor immediately because early detection is the key to a quick diagnosis. Have you told Bill?" questioned Mary.

"No, I needed some time," replied Toni.

"I will tell him tonight. I don't want him to worry. He is just getting back to normal. The strike was difficult for him. The union is still putting pressure on him to hire more people. He has

enough on his plate. When I saw his concern today I knew we needed to talk. I am afraid I might lose him if it's serious. How much pressure can a marriage take and still survive?"

"Bill loves you. Your marriage has already been tested and you both are stronger people. Whatever the outcome you have your family and your friends. We are here for you. Now go home and talk to your husband. Let me know when you get to the hospital tomorrow. I will be on duty if you need me," said Mary.

" I'll get Tommy while you compose yourself. Come out when you're ready."

Mary hugged her friend and left the room. Toni thought about how blessed she was. For the first time in a long time, she had friends who cared about her. She dried the tears. She had a loving and supportive family. Whatever happened she would be all right. Tommy could tell his mother had been crying. He knew she was not ready to discuss anything with him. They rode home in silence, each with their thoughts.

28

"Mom," said Tommy. "Thanks for taking John home from work.
I have some studying to finish. I'll see you in the morning.
Mom, I love you."
Tommy came over and hugged his mother.
"I love you too Tommy," replied his mom.
As soon as Toni walked into the room and saw her husband's
face she knew how much he loved her. She sat down on the bed
and tears streamed down. "I found a lump on my breast," said
Toni crying hysterically.

Bill pulled her into his arms and just held her. He would process
his pain later. For now, he just needed to be there for her.
Bill held his wife in his arms until she fell asleep. He knew the
family history. He tried not to panic. He knew that if it were
cancer it would devastate the family. He tried not to imagine the
worst. He wanted to wake her and ask what Mary had said, but he
didn't want to upset her. He crawled out of bed, dressed quickly,
and then went to the Humphries. He had to talk with somebody,
and Henry was his closest friend. He knew he should call but
didn't want to know if they were asleep. He needed answers from
Mary and support from Henry. He had never reached out to
friends before. He didn't want to seem
 weak or unable to handle things. One of the many things he
 learned from the strike was that he could discuss his problems
 with his friends without judgment. He didn't have to be

29

ashamed. He saw a light on in the living room when he pulled into the driveway relieved they hadn't gone to bed. Mary saw the car pull up in the driveway. Bill gets out and walks toward the front door. Mary opened the door before Bill knocked. She saw tears forming in Bill's eyes. She hugged him.

"I'm glad Toni told you," said Mary. "I'm glad you came. I'll go get Henry. He is in the den working."

"Mary," replied Tom. "Can we talk first?"

"Sure, I know you must have several questions. The first thing to do is make an appointment with your primary physician. They will perform a biopsy on the lump to see if it is cancerous or not.

In all probability, it is just a lump of tissue. If it is cancerous they will remove the lump and she will begin radiation treatment. The first thing though is to get her to the doctor. Do you have any other questions?" queried Mary.

No, what I want to do is to thank you for being there for Toni. I kept her from having friends during our marriage afraid that they would find out that she was an alcoholic. I loved her so much. I thought I was protecting her, but I was protecting myself and my reputation. I made so many mistakes. When men are mourning they turn to their job. I immersed myself in my work. I secretly blamed Toni for the death of our son. A part of me wanted her to go through the pain by herself. I shut her out and she turned to the bottle for comfort. We have friends now.

This is new for us. I needed to come over here. I realize that it's late. You didn't make me feel that I was intruding. You just opened the door. Thank you."

Henry walked into the living room and immediately sat down beside his wife. He knew something was wrong.

"Mary, why don't you get us some coffee while I visit with Bill," said Henry.

"I'll be in the den if you need me. I'll bring the coffee when it's done," replied Mary.

How are you holding up?" inquired Henry.

"Mary spoke with me after she talked with Toni. She thought you might need someone to talk with." Henry asked the question and

listened as Bill spoke of his fears and thoughts. He let him cry because he knew Toni would need his strength if she did have cancer. Bill was a good man. He had seen a change in him since Toni came home. He was happy. It had been a struggle for him. For the first time, he was opening up to the others. Henry knew this was difficult for him. He just sat in silence while he talked.

The doorbell rang. It was Toni. Mary walked to the door. Come on in the living room. I was just about to serve coffee. Toni's eyes met her husband's when she walked into the room. There was nothing in their eyes but the love they shared for each other. Mary put the coffee and some coffeecake on the table. It's all yours. Enjoy.

31

CHAPTER 4

District attorney Ronald Moran reviewed all the witness accounts of the day that Alan Bates committed suicide. The case had been debated on television news and internet radio. Activists were calling for the two boys who had tormented Alan to be tried as adults. States were rewriting bullying laws to include internet bullying and harassment. Children were committing suicide after prolonged verbal abuse and persecution by their peers. Alan Bates had murdered his father, and killed himself after Justin Houston and Carl Blevins teased him about his father's molestation. The outcome of this case would affect the futures of each of these young men.

Carl Blevins had been under a doctor's care since the incident. The court had appointed a counselor to evaluate him. He read the report again. Carl had been wetting the bed and suffering from nightmares. The court-appointed counselor said that Carl was ready to be questioned. He would interview both boys today. Carl would have to wait until an attorney was appointed for him but he wanted to have an opportunity to speak to Mrs. Blevins first.

Justin Houston had secured an attorney immediately. His family owned a restaurant and hotel and had retained Blake Donavan. He knew Blake's reputation. He would not let his client tell the truth. He would hide behind the 5th Amendment. He wondered how Justin was doing. The boy saw his classmate commit suicide in front of him. How was it affecting him? Would he be forced to live with the guilt for his part in the suicide?

Gladys knew what had happened to Alan Bates. Her son had relived the moment that Alan Bates had pulled the trigger over and over again. During counseling, he shared his description of the events. The counselor asked Mrs. Blevins to sit in on her session with Carl so that he could share his story with her. She knew this was difficult for her son, so she sat quietly and listened.

Carl began "Justin and I were surfing the internet and came across a website with sex offenders. We were curious to find out if there were any sex offenders in our area. We saw Robert Bates on the list, Alan's father. We had heard rumors that his father had molested him, but we didn't know if it was true. Justin said maybe we should let the other kids know that there was a pervert in our school. We were in the lunchroom when we ran into Alan. I yelled out that we heard his father was a pervert. I asked him if he got out of remedial class by giving sexual favors. I'm so sorry he cried. I wish that were the last time I talked to him. Maybe he wouldn't be dead."

His mother started to run to him, but the counselor stopped her, as she fought her own emotions wanting to do nothing more than to comfort her son.

Carl continued. "On the day that Alan killed himself, Justin and I

had been suspended. When we went to the locker to get our
things we saw Alan coming down the hall. He looked weird. His

shirt was hanging out of his pants and his hair hadn't been
combed. Justin hollered out at him that he was the pervert, and
we were getting suspended for letting everyone know. He said
maybe we should give it to him in the butt like his dad did. The
next thing I heard was the gunshot then Alan fell to the floor."
Carl could not hold back the flood of tears. The counselor
nodded and Gladys went to her son. She held him as the tears
flowed. It was difficult, but her son had finally told the truth.
Now the healing could begin. They could deal with his guilt.
Mrs. Blevins took her son home and put him to bed. He slept for
the first time. She sat in the chair beside his bed rocking back and
forth.

They entered the elevator and pushed the elevator button to the
6th floor. She could see a slight tremble of her son's hand. She
pulled her son closer to her and entwined his arm in hers. When
the elevator stopped, and the door opened Carl seemed to freeze
in that spot. His body stiffened. People looked at them,
seemingly wanting to push them out the door. She kissed her son
on the cheek and led him into the hallway. She stood with him a
moment and then led him into the district attorney's office.

Ms. Blevins,

"My name is Linda," said Moran's secretary.

"Mr. Moran will see you in his office." Carl can sit here with me."
"Carl I will be right back," said his mother.
Ms. Blevins sat down.

"I am Ronald Moran the district attorney. Before I interview your son I want to be sure that you have an attorney present. Have you retained an attorney?"

"No, we can't afford an attorney. Will we need one?" asked his mother.

"Mrs. Blevins, I can't answer that question right now because I have not had a chance to interview your son or Justin. I don't want to decide until I have reviewed all the facts. I will petition the court to appoint Carl an attorney before I question him. If you would like, his counselor can come with him. Linda will call you after an attorney has been appointed. You will meet with the attorney first, Then we will schedule an interview with you, Carl, and his attorney."

"Thank you, Mr. Moran.," said Gladys Blevins.

Carl and his mother went down the elevator and exited the building. The press was outside waiting on her. This was a juvenile case, so the children's identity was to be kept secret.

This was a small town.

"Ms. Blevins, has the court-appointed Carl an attorney? Are you aware that Blake Donavan is representing Justin Houston? Have the boys had a chance to talk?"

Ms. Blevins grabbed her son's hand, and they ran to the parking lot. While getting into their car they saw the Houston's. The boys looked at each other, seeming to understand each other's thoughts.

Gladys wondered if she should tell them to take the back

entrance into the office building. She thought about it for a minute then entered her car.

Justin had woken early. He had been thinking about what had happened. He knew Carl didn't have an attorney, so he might have to go to jail. He asked his parents to let Mr. Donavan represent both, but his parents said no. They didn't want him to speak to Carl. His attorney said it was best that they didn't talk until after the trial. Carl was his friend. He snuck and called him one day to see how he was doing. He told him he was still his friend. They were in this together. They weren't in this together. His attorney would blame Carl since he didn't have an attorney.

He was never to tell the truth.

Justin let himself drift back to the day Alan shot himself. He heard himself lashing out at him. Then he heard the gunshot as clear as if it were going off right in this room. He screamed. Then he doubled over sobbing loudly.

His mother heard him and came running into the room. He cried and cried as she sat holding him. He kept screaming. It's my fault. It's my fault. Susan called her husband. Titus came into the

36

room. Susan beckoned for him to sit down on the floor.

Susan's eyes met his. Our son needs to tell us the truth.

Justin began his account of the story holding nothing back. His

parents wanted to say something. They held their thoughts until

he finished.

Justin, I know you feel responsible. The best thing for you to do

is to do what Mr. Donavan is telling you. For now, do not tell

your story.

Mr. Houston called the attorney. He told him what had

happened. He said for now Justin was not to make a statement.

Mrs. Houston saw Carl as he entered his mother's car. She knew

she should say something to them, but she couldn't. If it were

her son's future or Carl's, God forgive her, she would protect her

son. Just before they exited the garage Carl's mother's car

slowed to a crawl.

She heard Gladys say

"The press is outside the office building waiting on you. Take the

side entrance on 5th street." She pulled out of the garage.

"Christians, I'm glad I'm not one."

The Houston's, their attorney, and Justin entered the office. Mr.

Donavan went to the desk for instructions.

"Mr. Donovan," said Linda. "It's good to meet you. Mr. Moran

will see you in the conference room to take your statement. You and Justin can go into room 224. His parents may be present if they want.

"Mr. and Mrs. Houston will sit in the waiting room. Can you show them the way?" asked Blake.

"Mr. and Mrs. Houston, come this way," pointed Linda.

They looked at him wondering why they were not coming with him and Justin. He reassured them that it was better for Justin. They did not like it, but let Linda lead them to the waiting room. Ronald and Blake shook hands, then he asked them to sit down.

Ronald began the questioning.

"Justin, how did you know Alan Bates?"

"He went to school with me, but we were not friends."

"Before the day he committed suicide did you run into him at the cafeteria?"

"Carl and I saw him in the cafeteria one day."

"Can you tell me what was said between you and Alan that day?"

Mr. Donavan interjected. "My client will not answer that question at this time. He will make a full statement if and when he is indicted."

Justin, we are leaving now.

Ronald knew the outcome before it happened. This was a fishing expedition. He wanted to know what he knew by the questions he asked. He was prepared for this response. He would see what happened in the next interview.

CHAPTER 5

Toni called Dr. Wade's office to make an appointment. The nurse looked at his schedule and advised her he didn't have an opening until next week.

"It's kind of an emergency," said Toni, so low the nurse could barely hear

her voice. "I have a lump on my breast."

"Mrs. Colbert, Let me talk to Dr. Wade and see if he can see you between appointments."

The nurse spoke with Dr. Wade, and he came to the phone. He had been treating Toni since she moved to Plains Estates. He knew her mother and sister died from breast cancer.

"Lauren, I'll speak to Toni myself. Pencil her in between 10:30 and 11:00. He picked up the phone.

"Toni, this is Dr. Wade I asked Lauren to slide you in between 10:30 a.m. and 11:0 0 a.m. tomorrow morning. Try not to worry. It could be a cyst, but we want to make certain. Toni, you won't be coming alone will you?" he queried.

"No, Dr. Wade, Bill will be coming with me. We talked last night." Toni knew he was wondering if she was hiding the lump from her husband.

Toni and Bill woke early. Her doctor's appointment was for 10:00 a.m., but she couldn't sleep. They had breakfast with the kids trying to keep things as normal as possible.

40

"Mom," Tommy asked, "Is everything ok with you?"

"I've been a little tired lately. I guess I'm getting old. I need to get more rest."

Tommy didn't believe her, but he wouldn't push her. He would wait until she was ready to tell the family. Most importantly he knew that his dad knew what was wrong. She wasn't going through it alone.

Toni and Bill walked into the doctor's office. They had a 30-minute wait. Toni began filling out the insurance papers while Bill fiddled with his phone. You can answer your phone if you need to. At that moment he knew Toni was asking him for his attention. She was still afraid to appear needy. She remembered that he used to get angry when she nagged him about needing him too much. He wanted her to be there for him, but occupy herself also. He laughed at the old Bill. He had come a long way.

Mrs. Colbert, the doctor will see you now.

Toni and Bill went into Dr. Wade's office.

"Toni, the first thing I want to do is examine you. Then if needed you will need to have a mammogram. Get undressed. The nurse will be in to take your vitals and get you prepared for the exam."

Bill watched as the nurse took Toni's vitals. Her blood pressure was a little high. He knew it was because of the stress of not knowing if she had cancer. There he had said it. They talked around it but never really said the word out loud.

41

Dr. Wade came into the room and began to examine Toni. He felt the lump and asked her a couple of questions. When Dr. Wade finished his exam he sent Toni to have a mammogram

completed. Toni, after you finish the mammogram it will be at least an hour and a half before I can compare the results with the previous results against today's. Bill, take Toni to lunch.

My nurse will call you when I have the results.

Neither of them was hungry. They decided to get some tea and sit outside in the courtyard. They were both silent, deep in their thoughts.

Bill thought back to when he met Toni. They were both in college, full of dreams. When they met he was dating another girl. Once he met her he knew she was his soul mate. Now she was facing another life crisis. The difference was that he was here with her. He was invested in their relationship mind, body, and soul.

Toni knew that Bill had stayed with her through her many stints in rehabilitation. She was a little afraid that this would be his final straw.

She knew he loved her, but she still worried about losing him. She turned to him, and he smiled. He took her hand, and they walked around the garden. There was no need for words.

They walked. Bill's phone rang. Bill started to turn it off, then realized it was the doctor's office. He answered the phone then turned to Toni.

"The doctor wants to see us," he said.

They entered Dr. Wade's office. They could tell by the look on his face that something was wrong.

"Toni, Bill, I want to schedule a biopsy first thing in the morning," said Dr. Wade.

"The test results are not conclusive, but I am concerned. Let's not jump to conclusions. The nurse will give you instructions for tomorrow. I'll see you in the morning."

Bill went to get the car while Toni talked to the nurse. Toni got into the passenger side. As they drove, a tear fell down her face. This scenario had played out with her mom and her sister. She was drunk through their pain. Now cancer had come knocking at her door.

Bill reached over and took her hand. They would get through this together.

CHAPTER 6

John went to the garage to find his dad.

"Dad, do you have time to talk to me?"

"Sure John," replied his dad. "Is something wrong? Is everything ok at school?"

"Dad, everything is good. I wanted to run something by you first and get your input. Sheltons is hiring a team lead. I wanted to apply for the job. What do you think?"

"John, you are an excellent student and athlete. You are a leader. You show initiative and have an excellent work ethic. Sheltons would be lucky to have you in a management role. Sheltons is a business. Management needs to have a flexible schedule and to work different hours. Are you willing to give up your mentorship or basketball to take a management position? Jose has worked around all of your schedules, but he has to consider the needs of the business first. Have you given this any thought?"

"Dad, I didn't think about having to give up anything. I want to be an engineer. I need a mentorship, so I can intern my senior year. I have an opportunity for a basketball scholarship if I continue to play well. I love the game. I am going to apply because it will give me experience interviewing. I will give it some thought though. I will talk to Jose about the schedule and the additional responsibilities. "

"John, I hope I didn't discourage you. I just wanted you to think

44

about it some more. I will support any decision you make if it doesn't affect your grades.

Maria looked up and saw her son coming through the door. He was all smiles.

"Jesus, what's up," exclaimed his mother. "You haven't come to see me at work for a long time. It must be important."

"Mom, Sheltons is taking applications for the team lead. I am going to apply."

"I didn't know you were interested in a management position with Sheltons. When did you make this decision?"

"I hadn't thought about it until the position became open. Mom, I need a 3.2 GPA. I am hanging on by my teeth, but John is helping me with chemistry. If I get a B- in chemistry I will have the GPA to apply."

"What about basketball" queried his mom.

"Mom, Let's face it. I spend most of my time on the bench. I am not going to get a basketball scholarship. Sheltons will pay for my education and give me a job while I attend school. If I go to school out of state, I can work for them during the breaks. My problem is that I have been a slacker. I am not always on time for work. Sometimes I hang out with friends and take the last bus to work. When I'm late I stay over but it causes other employees to take their break late or go home later. I watch John. He's always helping other people and taking on extra duties. Mom, my friends say that African Americans are lazy but if John

45

is an example they are hardworking people. I wish I

had been a better employee. I am turning over a new leaf. I am applying for the position, but if I don't get it I will step up so next time I will be ready. I want this Mommy. I do."

Maria smiled at her son. "Are you too old to hug your mother?

"Mom, wait until we get home, I am going to work now. I want to get there early so I can fill out the application."

Tommy had thought about the team lead position, but he knew it would conflict with basketball and academics. He also knew that something was going on with his mother. He had learned from his dad's mistakes. He would not put work before his family. They had been through enough.

Jesus and John got to work early. Both filled out the application for the team lead. During the shift, John noticed that Jesus was taking up the slack for slower employees. It seemed to him that Jesus had come to work with a new attitude, and it seemed to be working.

Jose advised both of them that he would set up interviews next week. That would give him time to review all the applicants. He would have a tough decision to make.

CHAPTER 7

Toni and Bill checked in at 6:00 a.m. They saw Mary come around the corner.

"I thought you guys could use some support. Henry will come by later," said Mary.

Toni and Bill both hugged Mary.

"Toni, it will be a simple procedure. Dr. Harris will draw out a sample of tissue and they will send it to the lab. If it is benign the procedure will be over. If it is malignant then they will perform a mastectomy or a lumpectomy. Have you and Bill discussed the options?"

'We wanted to talk with the doctor before we decided," answered Toni.

"I am praying for the best"

"Bill and Toni, You can come in now." Dr. Wade began. "Once we diagnose the tissue sample it will go to the lab. If it is cancer we will perform surgery. Toni because of your history I would opt for a mastectomy. It is your decision if the cancer has not spread. Once we get the results back I will need a quick decision. I will give you and Bill some time to discuss your options."

"Bill, I have been reading about my options. I can have a mastectomy which is a partial and reconstructive surgery. If it is cancer I want to treat it the best way possible so we can move on with our life. Bill, what are you thinking?"

"I'm thinking that I love you. Toni let's face it. You were never more than a B cup, I won't miss what I never had, he replied smiling. We will wait for the results and take Dr. Wade's recommendation. I want you back at home with our family."

Dr. Wade came in the door. "This is Dr. Harris. He will be performing the biopsy.

The tissue sample was taken to the lab. Bill waited with his wife. The lump was cancerous. Toni was immediately taken to surgery. When Bill got to the waiting area Mary was there sitting down.

She just sat and listened. It will be a while before they know anything. Dr. Wade will be with Dr. Harris. We signed the papers for Dr. Wade to do a mastectomy if necessary. We did not want to run the chance of the cancer returning. I'm scared Mary. I am so afraid of losing Toni again."

Dr. Wade and Dr. Harris walked into the room. Dr. Harris started the conversation.

" Bill the tumor was small, it had spread to the surrounding tissue. Because of Toni's history, the surgeon performed a partial mastectomy. We will run a series of tests to determine the most effective treatment. We will begin treatment tomorrow. We will choose between radiation and chemotherapy. Toni will be able to have reconstructive surgery after she heals."

Bill was elated. "Thank you both. When can I see my wife?"

"She will be in recovery for a couple of hours then she will be moved to a room."

"Mary, I need to call Betsy and inform her of what is happening. I will talk to the kids when I get home."

Bill made the call to Betsy. He told her that Mrs. Colbert was in the hospital and that he would talk to the children when he got home.

Toni was moved to a room. He went in and sat beside her bed. He laid his head on her lap and cried, thanking God for her recovery. Toni stirred and looked at her husband.

"Bill, whatever happened I am alive. I'm going home."

CHAPTER 8

Tad was determined to fight for custody of his niece, Tammy, against her adoptive parents. He knew he needed to convince his sister Alicia to fight for custody or there was no chance of his family getting custody of her.

He had met Tammy at his mother's house a couple of months ago. She looked just like her mother. She was beautiful. Alicia had gotten pregnant when she was 15 years old. She gave birth and then gave the baby up for adoption. Their mother felt it was best if Ted and Tad were never told about the pregnancy or the adoption. Both were already married, After the adoption her parents moved to New Hampshire, to protect Alicia's reputation. Tammy's adoptive parents, the Walkers, allowed Alicia to meet her daughter and spend time with our family. Alicia felt a sense of loyalty because they had embraced her and her husband Michael. The Walkers are good people, he had to admit. They had been blessed that Tammy had been placed with a loving family. Now it was time for her to be with her real family. For the families sake, he believed it would be better for Tammy to cut all ties with the Walkers

Tad decided to start with his parents. Alicia had already expressed her thoughts. She loved her daughter and would love to be a full-time mother to Tammy, but she would never betray the Walkers. Tad knocked on his mother's door. He could hear her coming to the door. It was hot and the screen door was locked so that a breeze could blow through the screen. His parents would die without installing central air although all the siblings had offered to pay for it.

"Tad, come on in," said his mother.

"I have been expecting you but on the other hand, I'm surprised to see you. Alicia is still upset with you. She had words for us too. I've never seen her so upset since we made her give up Tammy for adoption. Now you are jeopardizing her relationship with the Walkers and most importantly her daughter."

"Mom, I know that Alicia is afraid that she will lose all contact with Tammy but I've already talked with an attorney. Neither Donald nor his parents ever signed the adoption papers. Alicia was a minor. The decision to place Tammy for adoption was made by you and Dad. Alicia can say she was forced to place her child up for adoption against her will. They would have to,re-open the case. Donald had rights also. If he protests the adoption they still have to re-open the case. He wasn't allowed to keep his daughter. I have no legal rights unless Alicia seeks custody of Tammy. I have a private detective trying to find Donald. He could be of help to us in getting the adoption re-opened."

"Tad, I see you are pursuing this at any cost. Donald was scum. He got your sister pregnant and laughed in her face when she told him she was pregnant. He accused her of being a slut.

Bringing him back to town would only cause your sister pain. What if after you found him he decided to fight for custody of Tammy, What happens then? How would you feel if Tammy ended up with strangers" explained his mother.

"Mom, I do not doubt that Alicia would enter the custody

battle if Donald was fighting for custody of her daughter."

"So, you are going to use Donald to rope your sister into the battle."

"I believe God has given me a mandate to bring Tammy home to her mother."

"Son it was God that sent Tammy home with the Walkers. I used God as my reason for forcing Alicia to give her daughter up for adoption. Alicia was right. I was embarrassed. I wanted to hide her sin, so we sent her away to a home for unwed mothers. After she returned we moved her away from her church and her friends. You cannot hurt God's people. You cannot escape the consequences of your actions.

"Mom, I'm going to see Alicia. Maybe I can convince her to file for custody without bringing Donald into the picture.

Tad called his sister on his cell phone. He got the recorder.

Alicia saw his number come up and pressed ignore.

"Alicia, this is Tad. I know you're still angry with me, but I need to see you. We must talk. Call me when you

get this message."

Alicia and Ted got along great. Ted had even said that he and his wife would have adopted Tammy or kept her until Alicia was old enough to be a parent both emotionally and financially. He had children so he knew the importance of family. Ted could convince Alicia to see it his way.

Tad decided to visit Ted at his office. That way they would be on neutral territory. He rode the elevator and exited on the 10th floor of the Humana building. He had been to visit his brother many times but this time he went in with a little uncertainty.

"Marcia, Ted's secretary saw Tad standing at her desk. Marcia asked. "Is Ted expecting you?"

"No "spoke Tad. "Is he available? I need to speak with him."

"His next appointment is at 1:00 p.m. so he has an hour and 15 minutes for you. From the look on your face, it must be pretty serious. Go on in."

Tad knocked on the door and then went into the office.

"Marcia said I was free to enter," Tad said sheepishly.

"Come on in. For you to come to my office, you must be in trouble, or need a favor. Which is it? Let me guess. You know this is a small family and a nosy one. I have already spoken to Mom. She called me right after you left. She said you were planning to fight for custody of Tammy because let me think a moment. It must be because God told you Tad Brooks to split up a family, strip a little girl away from her adoptive parents, destroy your sister's relationship with her daughter, and bring back a man who jilted her when she got pregnant to get the upper hand and manipulate her into filing for custody of her daughter against her wishes. No wonder I find it hard to believe in your God. You always say you are a child of God. What are his other children doing, robbing banks, and destroying families for the greater good?"

"I can see this visit was wasted" replied Tad. "You mock God then you insult me."

"Hold on. I didn't mock God. I mocked you. Remember it was the same God that Alicia prayed to protect her child and place Tanny in a loving home. It was the same God that our parents say led them to give their granddaughter up for adoption because they were too embarrassed to bring the baby home. You people use God as an excuse to do what you want.. You mock God. The God I believe in is compassionate and merciful. His love does not permit me to destroy someone's family. He teaches me to love the Walkers and to thank them for rearing and protecting my niece from harm. He shows me that Alicia is blessed that they have shared this wonderful little girl with this family. They have shown more compassion and generosity toward this family than we deserve. No, I will not help you fight for custody of our niece. Please get out of my office before I slug your sanctimonious behind."

Tad could tell he would have a fight on his hands, but he was determined.

He made a call. "Richard, how is the search for Donald Cohen going? Keep me posted. He hung up the telephone and smiled.

CHAPTER 9

Rita woke up in pain. She had tried to sleep for hours. She felt hot. She didn't want to wake her parents if possible. The pain intensified. She had no choice but to call her parents. She pushed the beeper beside her bed that would notify her parents she was having pain. They had installed the beeper in case Rita was unable to reach her parents. Her parents immediately reacted as soon as the red light started flashing.

John got up and ran down the hallway. "Is Rita okay?" he yelled. His father quickly answered knowing he was upset. "Your mother is with her." As soon as the words came out of his mouth, his mom screamed.

"Call an ambulance. Her fever is 104. I am giving her oxygen." John immediately called 911. Her mom stayed with her until the ambulance got to the house.

"Mary, you ride to the hospital with Rita. I will stay with John."

"Dad, go to the hospital with mom. I have a job. I can certainly stay by myself. Just keep me informed."

As soon as the ambulance arrived Mary went to update the paramedics. She rode in the ambulance with Rita. Henry drove to the hospital. The ambulance barely beat him there. Rita was taken to the emergency room. They immediately wrapped her in warm blankets and tried to stabilize her.

Rita had been in crisis before, but this was different. She had a bad summer cold, but they were trying to take precautions. They knew if it turned into pneumonia the infection would cause her sickle cell symptoms to worsen.

Mrs. McKnight heard the ambulance and saw it stop at the Humphries' house. She called the house to see if John was okay. John picked up the telephone on the first ring.

"John, it's Jan McKnight. I saw the ambulance leave for the hospital and your dad leave alone. Are you okay? Do you want to stay with us?"

"No thank you, Rita was pretty bad. I want to wait here in case my parents call. I'm okay.

"John, if you want me to come over to stay with you while you wait call me."

John hung up the phone and fell to his knees. "God, this is a big one, but you have watched over this family, especially Rita for years. I know you are faithful and kind, so I leave my sister in your hands."

John gave thanks to God in advance. John plugged the hall phone into the outlet in his room. He didn't want to miss a call. Rita was stable for the moment. They put her in a room. She had pneumonia which caused the sickle cell symptoms to heighten. She was on oxygen, and they had administered drugs to fight the pneumonia. They had to be careful in treating the pain and fighting the illness. Mary entered the room, sat next to the bed, and took her daughter's hand. She would sleep for a while. Henry was waiting for Mary to come and bring him up to date.

She had gone to find out when Rita would be in her room. He looked toward the door and spotted Bill Colbert.

"Bill how is Toni holding up?" asked Henry.

"She's strong. They performed a partial mastectomy on her. They will be starting radiation treatment tomorrow. The tumor was small. Dr. Wade thinks that they got it all. Between you and me, Toni has a history of breast cancer in her family. I had prepared myself for a full mastectomy. This diagnosis comes as a relief. I'm going home to see my children. They know their mother is in the hospital, but I need to explain everything to them. I can tell they are afraid of losing her. Henry, are you waiting for Mary?"

"Rita was brought into the hospital. You know she has sickle cell anemia. Most times she's okay but this time she's suffering from pneumonia which makes the symptoms caused by her disease more painful. She's asleep now and Mary is with her. I have to call John. I'm sure he's waiting for my call.

"Henry, I am so sorry. I will let the children know that Rita is in the hospital. You know Tommy has quite a crush on your daughter. She is goal-oriented and a good influence on him." They both laughed.

"I've been trying to ignore the fact that my daughter is growing up" Henry joked.

"I'll get by to see Toni tomorrow. Get home to your children."

The telephone rang. John had drifted off to sleep. He picked up the phone,

"Hello," he said shaking himself out of his sleep.

"John, it's Dad, they have stabilized Rita for now. She is

sleeping.

John, Rita has pneumonia. Your mom is going to stay with her. I will be home after I see her."

"Dad, said John sleepily, "I prayed for Rita. She will be all right."

Henry was scared. He had never seen Rita this bad before. He put on a face and went to see his wife and daughter.

Mary looked drained. He could see she was concerned. No, that was an understatement. After 25 years of marriage, he knew his wife was afraid. She was a top-notch nurse. She was compassionate and giving. When it came to her family she was like a lion protecting her cubs. After John took her pills and overdosed nothing was given to her daughter without her finding out everything from side effects to complications. He knew she would not leave the hospital until her daughter was ready to go home. He leaned down and kissed his wife on the cheek.

Their eyes locked. They knew this was more serious than any time before.

Rita's eyes opened for the first time.

"Daddy, I'm in so much pain" Rita exclaimed. "Daddy, I think it's time."

She shut her eyes and gave in to the medication.

Henry led his wife outside the room and held her in his arms crying hysterically.

"Mary, Rita is wrong. It is not time yet."

Henry stayed with Rita allowing Mary to get some rest.

Although she tried she could not stay away from her daughter.

She sent him home to stay with John. Henry hesitated.

"Henry please, I need to know that my son is okay."

"Mary, call me if there is any change. I will be here in the morning."

Henry walked the long hallway holding back his tears. Rita was his baby girl.

"Lord, please let her be alright."

CHAPTER 10

Betsy had told the children that Mrs. Colbert was in the hospital. She informed them their dad would talk to them when he got home.

Terrence looked at Tommy.

"Is momma drunk again?" he asked. "Is she going back to rehab?"

"No Terrance, she is at the hospital where you go if you are sick. She's been looking tired lately and has been sleeping a lot lately. She tries to hide it with make-up, but it shows anyway. Let's not go to the dark side. Mom has been sober for a few years now. We need to give her the benefit of the doubt."

Debbie chided in. "I don't think she's drinking. I can tell when she's drunk. There would be bottles hidden everywhere. She would, Debbie made quotation marks with her fingers as she said, sleep all the time."

They all laughed. They knew that it meant she was passed out on the floor or the couch. When she was

sober, she was short-tempered and mean.

"She resented our intrusion into her drinking time" laughed Debbie.

The children were laughing but inwardly they were scared. At least with her drinking, they knew what to expect. She had never been physically sick.

They heard their dad come through the door. He looked tired and worried. It was worse than they thought.

"Guys, I'm glad that all of you are downstairs. Someone get Betsy Ask her to hold dinner. I'll be right back after I shower and change clothes."

Debbie went into the kitchen.

"Betsy, Dad said to hold dinner until after he speaks with us. Do you know what's wrong with momma? "

"No, sweetheart I don't. Debbie why don't you and your brothers set the table for dinner" she requested.

Debbie called the boys for backup.

Betsy put the food in the oven. She had been with the Colbert family since before they moved to Plains Estates. She was hired the first time Mrs. Colbert went to rehabilitation. She loved the family and was happy to be making the move with them. This family had been through so much. The last couple of years had been a happy time for the children. She had seen Mr. Colbert grow into a secure and confident man; He no longer needed to keep his wife in the kitchen. They were equal partners. He trusted her with the children. They shared in the decision-making when it came to education, chores, and discipline. Now Mrs. Colbert is in the hospital. She didn't mean to pry but she had overheard them talking. Mrs. Colbert had a doctor's appointment for a mammogram, then she returned to see the doctor. She didn't

want to assume anything. She would wait for Mr. Colbert

to tell her.

Bill stuck his head into the kitchen.

"Betsy, can you join us in the den? I want to talk to the family"

said Mr. Colbert.

Betsy sat down next to Terrance. He was the youngest. He

would need her support the most.

Bill began to talk. "As you know your mother is in the hospital.

Two weeks ago your mother felt a lump on her breast. After the

doctor examined the lump another doctor performed a biopsy. A

biopsy is when they take a tissue sample from your mother's

breast and examine it. When they examined the tissue they found

that your mother had cancer. They took out the lump and the

surrounding area. Your mother starts getting radiation treatment

tomorrow. She will recover. The treatments will be rough for

her, but the important thing is she will be all right. This is

emotionally difficult for your mother. Your grandmother and

Aunt Tessie both died as a result of having breast cancer. You

need to be as supportive as you can be. Everyone will need to

chip in and help. Betsy, when Toni comes home Mary

Humphries will help me hire a nurse. I see you frowning but you

will have enough on your plate taking care of the children and

the household."

"Can we go see momma?" asked Tommy

"Absolutely" replied Bill. I will take you tomorrow after school is out. I'll pick you all up from school. Betsy, can you serve dinner now."

Nobody ate much dinner. They were all having their thoughts. After dinner, they all ran upstairs to see what they could find out about breast cancer. They looked up the surgery, the treatment, and the success rate. After reviewing all the information they felt more positive about their mother's future.

Bill went back to the hospital to visit with his wife. First thing in the morning he would let his staff know that he would be working at home. He would put his vice-president Charles Schiller in charge on site.

CHAPTER 11

Dwight Summers was looking at the news. The boys' names
were protected because they were minors. One of them had an
attorney and the other boy would be appointed an attorney by the
court. He prayed for Alan's family. He also knew that the other
boy needed an attorney. No matter how atrocious their acts were
they had time to redeem their sins.

Dwight had petitioned the court to let him be the attorney for the
boy. He was waiting for an answer. Dwight was no newcomer.
He had practiced criminal law for 20 years. His heart went out to
this child. He had no right to judge him. He had told his
secretary to put the call straight through from the court.

Judge Rinehart reviewed the petition from Mr. Summers and the
case. It was an election year, and this was a hot topic. This case
had gone viral. The court could appoint an attorney for him, but
he deserved the best attorney the court could solicit. Mr.
Summers did not do pro-bono work. He took cases he could win.
He could have no opinion if this case went to trial, but he would
allow Dwight to represent Carl Blevins. He advised Virginia to
give the district attorney and Dwight Summers a call.

The phone rang. Dwight answered the line.

"Yes Sarah," asked Dwight.

"The judge's secretary is on the telephone."

Dwight picked up the blinking line. "Dwight Summers

speaking"

"Mr. Summers, the judge has honored your petition. District
Attorney Moran's secretary will call you and set up a meeting
with the boy before the questioning. He will send over the file."
Linda walked into Moran's office. "Judge Rinehart's secretary is
on the line. You should find this interesting."
Moran picked up the line.

"Mr. Moran the judge has answered a petition filed by Dwight
Summers to represent Carl Blevins. Please call the Blevins
family and Dwight Summers to set up a meeting between the
family and Dwight. It's probably better that they meet at his
office. Please send over the file so that he can review it before
the questioning."
This was a new twist in events. Why would Dwight Summers
petition the court to represent an unnamed minor? Dwight was
not a reputation seeker. He was a skilled criminal attorney who
did not work for the court. The case had not gone to the grand
jury. No arrest had been made but everyone expected a trial.
Ms. Blevins, Ron Moran. "An attorney Dwight Summers has
agreed to represent your son. You will need to meet with him
first thing tomorrow morning. His address is 3436 River Chase
Dr."
"Thank you, Mr. Moran. We will be on time,"

Gladys had taken an FMLA leave from work. Fortunately, she had 16 weeks of comp time due to her, so she was able to use that time before her leave started. She looked the attorney up on

the internet. He had been in practice for twenty years. He had only lost three cases and they were being appealed. Maybe my son would have a chance. She was not a religious person but maybe what they said was true. Maybe God did protect fools and children. The question is will he help or punish her son because she does not believe?

Ms. Blevins and Carl entered the law office. It was beautiful. The walls were tan, with maple furniture and comfortable chairs. This office was nothing like the district attorney's office. After her quick assessment, Gladys was ready to say thank you and leave. They could not afford this attorney.

Sarah buzzed Dwight to let him know that Carl and his mother were waiting for him.

Dwight came out and introduced himself to Ms. Blevins and Carl. He extended his hand. He was over 6 ft. tall, medium build, African American, with short hair, and brown eyes.

"I'm pleased to meet you, Ms. Blevins. Carl you and your mother come back to my office."

There was no picture on the internet. She didn't know if she felt comfortable with a Black man handling her son's case. Would he automatically lose if his attorney were Black? She wondered.

He had only lost three cases. A winning Black lawyer was better than a lawyer paid for by the state any day. She extended her hand.

"It's a pleasure to meet you, Mr. Summers. Can I ask you a question before we start?"

"Certainly, I have many questions for you" he answered.

"Why did you agree to represent my son?"

"I had a similar incident happen to me. I was much older at the time, but a fraternity brother was hurt badly. He ended up in the hospital. I, and a couple of friends were suspended for the semester, but God showed us grace and mercy. I returned to school graduated, and attended law school. I want to help Carl have a future."

Ms. Blevins thanked him for his help.

"Now let's get to work" Dwight instructed. "We meet with the district attorney tomorrow morning. Carl, I am your attorney. You will have to trust me. Tell me exactly what happened. Do not leave anything out."

Carl looked at his mother. She nodded her head.

Carl began his story "The first time I saw Alan was ...."

CHAPTER 12

The staff was shocked when Bill called his executive team and asked them to meet in his office at 8:00 a.m. It was Monday. There was no scheduled meeting until 9:00 a.m. They only had bad thoughts in their mind. They had recently gone through a strike. Were they facing layoffs now?

"Everyone please take a seat. Thank you for coming on such short notice. During the next few weeks, I will be working at home.."

They felt relieved their job was not in jeopardy, but they were concerned. This was unique for Bill. He worked long hours and was a workaholic.

"Charles, I trust you to handle things on-site for me. Toni has been diagnosed with breast cancer. She had a mastectomy yesterday and we are waiting on her treatment schedule. Anything that needs approval please send it to Charles. If he needs my signature, he will email me and send the papers by carrier. I need to be available to my family until Toni gets through radiation and then chemo. I know you can handle everything. I will be in the office once a week. We will review all reports at that time. Please have them on time so I can review them before the meeting. I could not take this time if I did not trust this staff."

"Bill," said Charles, "thank you for having confidence in us. We will not let you down."

"I have to get to the hospital. Please handle the 9:00 a.m. meeting. I have emailed you all of the reports. I'm sorry this is such short notice. I didn't anticipate the swiftness of events."

"Bill, take care of Toni. I will only call you if I need to. I will cc you on everything because I don't want you worrying about anything else."

Charles met with the staff at 9:00 a.m. They reviewed all the reports and gave Charles their support. Each foreman met with his team so they would know what was going on. The union had already informed them that Henry's daughter was in the hospital in a coma. They were like a family and the news was devastating to them. The best thing they could do to show their respect for these two men was to pray for them and do their job the best they knew how. They would pull together to make sure everything went smoothly. Mr. McKnight was a good friend to both Bill and Henry. The Colberts and the Humphries had been there for Robert Hayden when his son was diagnosed with Down syndrome helping the workers keep affordable health insurance. Bill Colbert had changed since his wife had returned home. He was a different man. They would be in prayer for both families. "Toni, I'm sorry I had to go to the plant to talk with the staff. I put Charles in charge on site. I am going to work at home. So that I can spend more time with you and the children."

"Bill, you didn't have to. The plant needs you."

"No Toni, you and the children are my lifeline. The plant is my job. It took me a long time to realize that fact. My life at the

plant is better because of you. You made me a better person. Your compassion has become mine. Your strength made me stronger. I no longer have anything to prove to the world. I just want to prove my love to you. I love you. I want to be here with you. You will be begging me to go back to work before long. The nurse gave Toni some pain medication. Bill plugged in his computer and began to work. As promised Charles copied him on the morning meeting and reports. He could relax and take care of his family. He received an email regarding a part shortage. He forwarded it to Charlie. When Charlie received the email he handled it immediately. After all, he was trained by the best.

CHAPTER 13

Dwight picked up Carl and his mother to take them to the district attorney's office. He believed that Carl and Justin were cruel and mean but they were not the primary cause of Alan Bates's suicide. They did not intend for Alan to take his life. They were reckless with their words. They never thought about the consequences of their actions. He believed as Ms. Blevins did that the two boys had contributed to Alan's pain. Carl would tell the truth about what he said to Alan during their two encounters. If he hid the truth, the jury would think he showed no remorse for his actions. He was preparing his client for the worst possible outcome. They stepped into the elevator and once again pushed the 6th floor. Dwight went to the reception area while the Blevins waited for directions.

"Good morning Mr. Summers, Ms. Blevins, and Carl. DA Moran will see you in the conference room" said Linda.

Dwight called Carl and Ms. Blevins to follow him. DA Moran stood up and shook each person's hand. Please sit down at the table.

Dwight spoke first

t." At this time Carl Blevins will make a statement of his two encounters with Alan Bates"

Carl told everything that happened between him and Alan.

Moran asked a few questions, then he let them go. Ms. Blevins thanked Dwight when he took them home.

"Moran will take this to the grand jury. This is a controversial issue. It will be tried in court first. Afterward, laws preventing bullying will get stricter,, so I expect there to be formal charges. My staff will be prepared in case. Let's not get ahead of ourselves. We'll wait for their decision."

The case was all over CNN and other news shows especially internet radio. Some blamed the parents, his father, the boys, and even Adam himself. He listened to all the views preparing to launch his case.

Moran reviewed all the witness statements. He knew without a doubt that these boys were partially responsible for this young boy's death. Were they an accessory to his death? The answer would be yes. Win or lose this case would send a message. The charge would be harassment, verbal abuse, taunting, and intent to harm. The charges would carry 1-5 years in a juvenile detention center. The charges were felonies.

The attorneys were called and given the charges. They were to bring the boys to court with their parents. They would be released in their parents' custody. A preliminary hearing would be held to evaluate the evidence. The hearing would be held in 3 days. Dwight called the Blevins and arranged to pick them up and bring Carl into the courthouse. Blake called the Houston's. He would meet them at the courthouse.

The arraignment was quick. The charges were read. The boy's

attorneys pled not guilty. After the plea was entered the boys
were released to their parents. Because this was a juvenile case
the press was not allowed to be in the hearing.

Mrs. Bates stayed as far away from the courthouse as possible.
She prayed for the two boys, her son's persecutors; after it was
over she would move her daughter to her hometown in Georgia.
One can never run from your past, but her daughter deserved not
to be punished for the sins of her father.

Since Carl had told the truth he was able to sleep. He was still in
counseling, but he had returned to school. He was still afraid of
what might happen to him, but he didn't live in fear of people
discovering the truth. His mother came in to tell him goodnight.
She prepared her chair.

Carl looked at her and said

"Momma you can go to bed tonight. I have been praying to God
and everything will be okay. I asked Mr. Summers why he was
representing me. He said sometimes the Holy Spirit speaks to
you. He said every time he heard someone discussing the case
there was a tug of his heart, an inner voice. He said no matter
what, one must be obedient to the Holy Spirit because it is a gift
from God to lead and direct your life. I asked him how I would
know when the Holy Spirit speaks to me. He said it is your

conscious that stops you before you do something wrong. Sometimes you are too angry to listen. That slight hesitation is the Holy Spirit trying to get your attention. You have to be still and listen. He said when we both agreed to tell the truth his decision to represent me was affirmed by God. 'Son, I have never prayed in my life. My life has been difficult. No one was there to help me. My parents turned away from me. They were embarrassed. There was no God that came to my rescue. It was the state that provided welfare, food stamps, and Medicaid. It was Job Corps that provided me with an education and a skill. It was my strength that reared you. If believing in God gives you comfort then I am happy for you. I cannot embrace this Holy Spirit, but I thank the Holy Spirit who brought Dwight Summers into our lives. Goodnight son."

Justin went straight to his room. He had seen Carl in court. He had an attorney, and he didn't look scared. His parents were with him and their hotshot attorney. He felt removed from the entire procedure. He entered a plea and then he was released to his parents. His parents talked to his attorney and then they took him home. His parents owned a hotel and restaurant. They quickly dressed and went to work. Since the event, which is what it was called in his household, he had been tutored at home. He would be going to a private school in the fall. Oh, I forget, if I'm not in a detention center. My parents were sure they could buy me out of this mess. His mom came in to kiss him good night. She kissed him, touched his arm, and shuttered. She could not think about losing her son, not for a minute let alone 5 years. Her son thought she was aloof and detached. She had four miscarriages before he was born. There was an inner fear of losing him. It made her keep herself emotionally detached to protect herself. Now she wondered if her detachment had led her son to this cruel behavior. Was it her fought? Had she destroyed her son?

CHAPTER 14

Jose had posted a job for a team lead. It was time for Sheltons to begin its mentorship program in this area. He had four applicants to review for the job.

The first candidate was Daniel Sardis. He had been with the company for two years. He wanted to be in management, but he didn't want to do the work. He had just had his 2nd annual review and his work ethic had not changed. He remained an adequate employee. He showed no initiative and did not follow instructions. He was tardy all the time and his grades were not good. He immediately put his application aside.

The next applicant was Donna Sellers. Donna was a good worker. She showed initiative and had wonderful customer service skills. Her attendance was near perfect. Her drawback would be her grades. She had a C average. She needed a 3.2 and her average was a 2.6. Donna knew her average was too low to apply but he encouraged her to apply. He wanted to give her experience interviewing and map out an action plan for her. In time he hoped she would meet all the qualifications. He felt like she could have a future with the company.

John was the perfect candidate on paper. He had a 3.95 grade point average. He always took the initiative to take on extra duties and help the crew. He was good with the customers. John wanted to be an engineer. He was also an excellent basketball player. His question would be could John devote the time needed to the store with his other interest?

The last applicant was Jesus Ramirez. Jesus had a GPA of 3.2, but his performance was average. The last few days he had stepped up his game. He had an attitude adjustment. He was taking on tasks without being asked, arriving early rather than late, or just on time. This interview would be interesting. His question would be if this were a temporary adjustment or a change of work ethic. Jose called the applicants to schedule the interviews.

The phone rang. John hurried to answer it. Rita was in a coma. He thought it might be his dad picking him up.

"Hello," he answered.

"John, it's Jose Gonzales. I called to set up your interview for the team lead."

"Mr. Gonzales, I was hoping I could interview later in the week. If that's not possible I will have to withdraw my application."

"John, do you have practice?" he asked.

"No, my sister is in the hospital. She has sickle cell anemia. She has pneumonia and is in a coma. I need to be at the hospital with her."

"John, I am so sorry. Is there anything I can do for you?"

"Jesus volunteered to take my shift tomorrow if it's ok with you. We were going to call you later."

"John, I am going to call Jesus next. I will confirm it with him. Let me know if you need additional time off."

"Thank you, sir, I should be back to work by Friday. Can I get back to you later this week?"

"Of course, you can John. I will call and see how your family is doing. My prayers will be with you and your family."

Jose called Jesus. John was a good young man He had his priorities straight.

Jose's parents had died when he was 11 years old. He was reared by his grandmother. Jesus had stepped up to the plate by agreeing to cover John's shift. He began to think of Jesus as a potential leader.

John heard the phone ring and grabbed it. "Hello"

"John, it's me, Jesus. Jose said it was okay for me to cover your shift."

"He told me when he called. You are interviewing for the team lead position" he queried.

"Yes, my interview is going to be tomorrow after school. When's he going to schedule your interview?" he asked.

"Later in the week so hopefully Rita will be better by then."

"My mom and I will pray for her."

"Thanks, Jesus. That's my dad honking the horn. He's picking me up to go to the hospital.

CHAPTER 15

Bill picked up the kids from school.

"How is mom dad?" Tommy asked.

She has some pain & discomfort but seeing you, your brother, and your sister will cheer her up. She misses you.

They hesitated before hugging their mother. They didn't want to hurt her.

"It's alright," she said as she reached to hug each one of them, "This side is not painful. Sit and tell me about your day. The children started chattering as usual, interrupting each other. Terrance was telling a story about the class mouse escaping and running around the room. One girl jumped on the chair and started squealing. I held the mouse up to her and told her not to worry because I had him by the tail. She squealed even louder. Everyone including Toni started laughing. "You would have thought she would have been happy that I caught him," said Terrance. They laughed even more.

The nurse came in to change Toni's dressing. Bill could see that she was in pain and beginning to get tired.

"Come on kids say goodbye to your mother. After her dressing is changed and she takes her pain medicine she will fall straight to sleep" said their father.

Toni thought about Terrance and smiled. God had blessed her with the joy and laughter of her family. Now she would rest.

"Dad is mom going to be alright?" asked Tommy. "She was

trying to be brave for us, but she was in pain."

"She will continue to have pain until the swelling has gone down. The chemotherapy will be difficult for her. I will be working at home so that I "can be there for you guys and mom" he replied.

"Dad" exclaimed Debbie. "You have never stayed home from work. This is serious. Is there anything else we need to know?"

"I have told you everything. We have a rough road ahead but this time We will walk this road together. I will not be missing in action."

He said almost silently.

"Dad, the term is emotionally unavailable," she said laughing as he pulled into the driveway.

"You 'all get washed up for dinner. I will talk with Betsy," said their dad.

"Betsy"

"Yes, Mr. Colbert" she answered.

I will be working at home until Mrs. Colbert has finished her chemotherapy and recuperated. I'll use the study for my office. I am having a separate phone line put in that room. You don't have to answer that line. It will be a company line. It will also ring at my secretary's desk. She will take the messages for me. Most of the messages will be forwarded to my staff. Carrie will

make me aware if it is an issue that only I can handle" he
explained.

"The line was put in this morning "Mr. Colbert,"
Betsy told him.

"Carrie said, "When you get in call her to make sure everything
was set up correctly."

Carrie, Bill Colbert. Thank everyone for getting everything
completed so quickly.

"How is Toni?" she asked.

"She is doing as well as expected"

"We are praying for your family. Bill, where two or more are
gathered prayers are answered. "

"Please forward everything I don't have to handle personally to
Charles" explained Bill. "Carrie, thank you."

Bill got ready to join the children for dinner. Then he and
Tommy would go back to the hospital. Tommy was older. He
had questions he wanted to ask his mother. He had always been
her protector. He needed to be again.

John gathered his things and went to the car.

"Hey Dad, how's Rita doing? John asked his father

"Not much better son. She's still on oxygen and she is in a coma.
Your mother said that the pneumonia and the pain from sickle
cell have taken their toll, and the coma is giving her body time to
rest. Your mother is watching over her. I came home earlier and
picked up some clothes for your mother."

Are you hungry?" he asked John,

"No, Dad, I'm not hungry. I want to see Rita. I can wait to eat as

long as it isn't hospital food.

When they entered the third floor nursing station they saw Mary

at the desk. Her head was down so no one could see her tears.

When she saw her husband, she ran into his arms sobbing

relentlessly. She cried until her body collapsed against his.

"Baby, her husband spoke gently to her, you have to get some

rest. Patrice, please take my wife somewhere that she can lie

down. John and I will stay with Rita."

John and his father sat by the bed and talked to Rita. John

reached out and held her hand.

"Dad, Can I be alone with Rita for a while? You go check on

Mom."

John began talking. "Rita, I figured you wanted to be alone with

your big brother. I didn't want to get all mushy with Dad in the

room, I love you, Rita. You are my little sister. I am supposed

to protect you. You are also my friend. We've been there for

each other through the good and the bad. You are there when I

need to talk. You are funny and super smart. God has so many

wonderful things in store for you. You will be the doctor who

will find a cure for sickle cell anemia so that other children

won't suffer. I know what will bring you back. Tommy has a

crisis. You are always there for him when he needs you. I know you two have a thing for each other. Maybe his voice will wake you up. John called Tommy's cell phone.

"Tommy, John, Where are you?"

"I'm on my way to the hospital to see my mom. Do you think I

can see Rita?" he asked,

"Tommy, she is in a coma, but you can see her" he answered.

Tommy went to see his mom first and then he went to see Rita.

She had stabilized so she could have visitors.

Tommy sat down to talk with her and hold her hand.

"Rita, I am still waiting for you so we can be more than friends. You are a beautiful girl with an amazing heart. I need you to hold on for our future. No matter what our age is we are destined to be together. I will let you sleep now, but I will be back tomorrow if I can.

"John, will you call me and tell me how she's doing?"

"Sure Tommy, I know how you feel about her."

Bill, Henry, and Mary came into the room,

"Bill will give you a ride home John. I am going to stay with your mother. I know you have to work tomorrow. I know what you are thinking but you also have a responsibility to your employer. I will call you if there is a change in her condition. Rita would want you to go" his dad insisted.

Jose called and I asked his permission for you to have your cell phone with you at work in case of an emergency. He said it was fine so please don't abuse it. Jose is a good man. You are lucky to have him as a boss.

"Tommy, John come on, let's get something to eat," said Bill.

Tommy had been off for a few days. He needed to get his schedule and talk to Jose. Nathanial and Jose were both working tonight. They saw Jose helping out in the front. Nathaniel and

Jesus was working the grill and fries. It was near closing and the store was not busy. "Let me get your orders and then Nathaniel and I will come and sit with you for a minute."

Jose had shared the news about John's sister with Nathaniel and Greta.

Jose called to the back. "Jesus, can you cover the front counter?"

Maurice came back from break and took over in the back."

"Sure, Mr. Gonzales. John, Tommy, how are the two of you holding up?" asked Jesus.

John answered quickly. "As best we can but I'm sorry I haven't been available to tutor you."

I talked to my counselor. She assigned me a tutor. I didn't want to bother you while your sister was so ill. Tommy, how is your mom doing?"

Jose and Nathaniel looked up. He had no idea Tommy's mom was having problems. Tommy looked at Jose.

"My mom has breast cancer. She's still in the hospital. She

85

begins treatment this week. She'll be coming home soon we

hope. I came to talk with you and get my schedule."

"Do you need some extra time off?" Jose inquired.

"No, my dad is working from home. We have a housekeeper, and

my father is hiring a nurse. I want to work. I need to buy a

present for a friend."

John looked at him and smiled.

Jose went over to speak with Mr. Colbert.

"Mr. Colbert, I am sorry to hear about your wife. I know it must

be difficult for you and your family. If Tommy needs time off just

have him call before the schedule is made out.

"Thank you, I can see our orders are ready. We better go so I can

get back to the rest of the family."

Nathaniel had to come in tonight because the store was short-

staffed. Two of the employees had called in. He looked at these

two young men. He knew about John's sister, but he had no clue

about Tommy's mom being in the hospital. One boy had called in

with a personal issue. Samantha was 17 with a child and going to

school. She couldn't get a sitter. He needed to know more

about his employees and their lives. He assumed for the most

part they were young, carefree, and just calling in and being

irresponsible. He thought Jesus was a slacker. Since applying for

the team lead position he has shown true leadership skills. He

had been wrong about him from day one. Maybe if he had

encouraged him more he would have shown these characteristics much sooner than later. He didn't know how, but he would become an active participant in this team instead of an outsider looking in.

Henry turned the key in the lock and opened the door.

"Dad, I heard you come in. How is Rita?"

"She is slowly showing signs of coming out of the coma. We have to keep praying and trusting God. John, have you been able to complete all your assignments? I know you are worried about your sister."

"

Dad, I'm okay. I miss Mom but I know she has to be with Rita. She reads my papers and lets me run ideas by her."

"John, I am not your mother, but I am here for you. I can read your papers. Why don't we take a walk like we used to do and talk and catch up on things?"

"Let me put my sneakers on first then I'll be ready. Speaking of reading papers, you can read this one while I get some shorts on" teased John.

Henry laughed. "I walked right into that one, didn't I? I've been set up."

John laughed and kept walking.

Tommy sat in his room crying. Debbie walked by the room and heard him sobbing. She knocked on the door. "Hey brother can I come in?" she asked.

Tommy didn't answer so she opened the door and sat down on

the bed beside him.

"Tommy, Mommy is going to be all right. The chemotherapy will be hard for her, but she will be okay" she said comforting her brother.

"I went to see Rita. Debbie, she just slept. I talked to her, but she didn't move. I know the two of you are close and with Mom in the hospital, I didn't tell you that she is in a coma."

Debbie held back her tears. She needed to be there for her brother.

For the first time, I cried for Momma because I was trying to be brave. I was crying now because I couldn't cry then. I care for Rita a lot. I know it doesn't make sense because I am only 15. We have been friends for a long time. I trust and respect her. She has always been my sounding board when things are bad. Without her, I feel like half of me is missing. I need her to wake up and be there for me. I need her to wake up knowing that I am there for her. I depend on our friendship."

Debbie leaned down and hugged her brother." I love you, Tommy. I know it's not the same, but I am here for you until Rita is better. Then I will gladly put you in her hands."

"I love you too sis."

The telephone rang in the middle of the night.

Henry, it's Mary, Rita is awake. They will run tests tomorrow morning but everything seems okay. She's sleeping now. I keep waking her up to make sure she doesn't slip back into the coma."

"Mary, Let us pray. We thank you, God, for this miracle. We praise your name. In you, we put our trust. It is you that we praise. Amen.

Mary, get some sleep yourself. I will be there first thing in the morning. Goodnight sweetheart. I love you."

Henry got on his knees and sang praises to God.

He went into John's room and woke him up with the news. John thanked God and then he texted Tommy. Rita is awake.

Tommy heard the text. He hoped it wasn't some girl that had

gotten his number. He started not to look then he picked up the phone and read it.

Thank you God for bringing her back to me. He turned over and fell back to sleep. He would tell Debbie first thing in the morning. He got out of bed and ran to Debbie's room.

"Debbie, Rita's awake" he screamed. His dad looked into the room.

"Dad, Rita's awake."

"I think everybody on the block knows Tommy. Get some sleep. God is working these things out. God, how awesome is he?"

CHAPTER 16

Alicia had ignored Tad's messages until she had a chance to speak to Ted and her parents. Both agreed that she could not ignore his messages, because it would only make him more determined. He was looking for Donald Cohen, Tammy's biological father. As far as she knew he never knew he had a child. Once she went away to have Tammy he was forgotten in her mind. He had used her. She had given him her most precious gift, her virginity. He had laughed in her face and called her a slut. She knew he left town after high school and went to college. He never came back to town. It was as if he just disappeared. What would she do if he tried to take her daughter from the Walkers? She knew she would have to enter the fight. Alicia decided to invite Tad over to see what he was up to. She had to stay one step in front of him.

Alicia called Tad and got his voicemail. She left a message.

"Tad, I'm sorry that I didn't get your message. Why don't we get together for lunch? Call me when you get this message. Tad did not return her message and his secretary said he was out of time. She smelled trouble. Where was Tad? What was he up to now?

Detective Richard had called Tad on Wednesday morning. He had a firm lead on Donald Cohen. He was married with twin daughters. He owned an accounting firm. He was an upstanding citizen and sat on the board of the local United Way. He lived in

San Francisco California.

Tad pondered the information over in his head. He would be a good role model if he decided to fight for custody of Tammy. Maybe the family was right. Maybe he didn't need Donald to win this battle. He thought about it for a minute then decided to contact Donald.

"Richard, give me the number and I will take it from there." Tad insisted.

"Here's all the information including the profile of the Walkers. They are wonderful people, and your niece seems happy. Do you want to pursue this angle?" he asked.

"I can't reason with my sister or my family. Tammy needs to be back with our family. I have prayed and I know that I am right." "I'd hate to have you for a brother. I'll send you my bill."

Tad reviewed the report and made a phone call to Donald's office. Without disclosing any information he made a 3:00 p.m. appointment for tomorrow.

Tad told his wife he had to go out of town on business and prepared to leave for the airport. He set up an appointment with one of his clients so the trip would not be in vain.

Tad had a moment of conscious before getting on the plane. He called Alicia's number then disconnected it before she came. It was better that she didn't know that she had found Donald.

Tad caught a cab to the hotel. He would see his client in the morning and then Donald in the afternoon.

91

Alicia knew trouble was brewing so she called the Walkers.

"Hello," Nancy it's Alicia. We need to talk. Can you and John get away for a couple of hours? It's pretty important."

"Alicia, I will see if the children can stay at the McKnight's and we will be over in an hour."

"Hello," "Jan it's Nancy. Do you mind if the kids come over for a while? Alicia wants to talk to us."

"Send them over when you are ready to leave. Nothing's wrong is there?"

"I don't know yet, but we need to find out. Thanks, I'll send them over. We want to be late."

Nancy hung up the telephone and joined John in the study.

"Alicia called. She wants you and me to come over to her house. She needs to speak to us. Jan is going to watch the kids for us. I knew the ax would fall but not this soon. God help us." "Nancy, you are overreacting. It's probably nothing to do with custody of Tammy. Maybe they are having another child. Let's stop anticipating trouble and see what they have to say."

Nancy called out to the children. "Tammy, Jonathan, "your dad and I are going out. We are going to drop you off at the McKnight's. Get your things."

Tammy and Jonathan loved going over to the McKnights. They always had fun. Now that Rita would be coming home soon, and Mrs. Colbert was recovering maybe we could all play together at the park. They wanted things to get back to normal.

Men were so naïve. She knew that Tad was a snake. He had his claws in Tammy as soon as he saw her. He was overly polite, a

man of God, oh my.

Tad was slightly early for his appointment. He didn't know what exactly to say. Donald might throw him out just like he laughed at Alicia when she told him she was pregnant. He had come into his office, a stranger to ask him to reopen the adoption for a child he had never met.

Donald's receptionist advised Tad that he was ready and could step into his office.

"Mr. Brooks, how can I help you? You are from Salem Oregon. I grew up there."

Donald had looked Tad up on the internet so he would be prepared. He owned a steel manufacturing plant. He had clients across the country and globally. He was certain he had a CPA so what did he want?

"Donald, my visit is more of a personal nature. My sister is Alicia Steele formerly Alicia Brooks."

He gave Donald time to remember the name.

Donald would never forget that name. He was 15 years old and having fun. He ran a line on all the girls. Some fell for it some didn't, but it didn't matter. He was popular and a football player. If one turned him down there was always another one waiting.

Alicia was different. She was a virgin. He didn't know. He thought she knew the deal. Nobody wrapped it up in those days. You just went with the flow. When she told him she was pregnant. He flipped out. He didn't know what to do. He and his father went to talk to her and her parents They said she had left

town. After she left town his father told him it was nothing he could do about it. If she contacted the family he would do the responsible thing. She never contacted him, so he assumed either she wasn't pregnant, or she gave the baby up for adoption. Every now and then he would think about the incident, and wonder if he had another child. He told his wife before they married. If there was a child he didn't want any surprises. Now in his office was Alicia's brother. Did she send him here?"

Tad started again. "Alicia has no idea that I am here. Alicia had the baby and gave her up for adoption. We never knew. My mom and dad moved away. Recently Alicia and her husband Michael moved back to Salem and contacted the adoptive parents. That's how I met Tammy. He pulled out her picture. Don't get me wrong the Walkers are wonderful people and I am eternally grateful that they adopted Tammy. However, Tammy belongs to her biological family. Alicia will not seek custody from the Walkers because they allow her and the family to see Tammy. The reason I am here is because when Tammy was born you were denied your parental rights. I want you to reopen

94

the adoption so that Alicia will be forced to fight for custody.
As the biological parent she would win." After hearing his
story, Donald looked at him strangely. "You came here hoping
that I would reopen the adoption case and
fight for custody so that Alicia would enter the battle and take
custody of my daughter." He stared at her picture. She was
beautiful. She looked like her mom but with his lips.

"Tad, I have no intention of playing into your game. What
makes you think that I wouldn't get custody or that the Walkers
might win and cut Alicia off from Tammy altogether? You have
made a grave mistake Mr. Brooks. I need you to leave my
office."
Tad left his card with the receptionist.
Donald sat in his chair absorbing everything. He called his wife
and then hung up. He needed to go home and prepare her for this
himself. No telling what Tad would be up to next.
Tad left disappointed. He would give Donald time to think about
it. He left her picture with him hoping he would change his
mind. He would wait for his call.
Alicia led Nancy and John into the room. "I see you're anxious
so I will begin." Alicia looked at Michael for support. "Tad is
trying to get me to re-open the adoption and fight for custody of
Tammy. Don't worry we know that Tammy is happy with you.
We are blessed that you have allowed Tammy to share in our

95

lives. There is a bigger problem. My brother is looking for Tammy's biological father, Donald Cohen. He is hoping that Donald will re-open the adoption, fight for custody then I will fight for custody myself. I haven't spoken with Tad because he is out of town. I have no idea if he found Donald or what might happen. I want you to know that I am on your side and will fight with you if we have to."

Nancy sighed, "John I told you that Tad was up to no good. Alicia, I have already spoken to an attorney in case we need

one."

John looked at Nancy. "Why didn't you tell me?"

The women looked at each other and laughed. "Men, They both said together."

John and Nancy rode home in silence. They knew that if they had to fight for their daughter. they would be prepared.

John broke the silence. "Nancy, after the children are in the bed you can tell me what the attorney said about our chances."

Nancy knew that she was not fighting this battle alone. Alicia's words were his wake up call.

Donald went in the back door. He knew Casey would be fixing dinner. She looked at him and knew he was upset. She just sat down to listen.

He pulled a picture out of his pocket and gave it to her. She looked at the picture and knew it was his daughter. She came over and sat on his lap.

She asked him how he found out. He relayed the story to her down to every detail. She was amazed that anyone could be so cruel.

"Casey, I will not play his game, but I want to meet my daughter. If the Walkers allowed Alicia and her family to meet her maybe they would let her be a part of our family."

Casey hugged her husband. He had lived with the uncertainty for years. Now he knew and he could let go of the pain. He had a daughter, and she was brought up by loving parents. Now if he could just meet her.

Donald went to call his dad. "Dad, I am sending over a picture of your granddaughter. The Walkers adopted her. His parents still lived in Salem. His father received the email with the scanned attachment. His mother had passed two years ago. "Son, it's time you came home to meet your daughter."

"I hope I can dad. It would be a miracle."

Alicia felt better after talking to the Walkers. They would fight together. Her daughter would remain in the home she grew up in. Together they would make sure it happened.

CHAPTER 17

Jose had postponed the interviews until today because the staff had been short. He also wanted to interview applicants back to back. He invited Nathaniel to sit in while he interviewed each candidate.

He interviewed Daniel first. After Daniel completed the interview he explained that to be a team lead one had to be punctual, show initiative, and be a leader. Daniel, you are exceptionally good with the customers. Your attendance record is poor, and you tend to avoid work. I have kept you on staff because you have it in you to be a leader one day.

Daniel, here is a chart. In one column write the things that you excel at completing. In the other column put the things that need to improve here at Sheltons. The bottom column lists the qualities I look for in a team lead. When you finish your list see how many of those qualities match the qualities needed for the job.

As you improve your attendance, initiative, leadership skills, and grades check them off. When you complete the qualifications, we will consider you for a team lead position. Jose stood up and shook his hand.

"Thank you for coming in today," said Jose.

"We look forward to interviewing you next time." Nathaniel stood and shook Daniel's hand.

Jose and Nathaniel interviewed Donna after Daniel. Nathaniel, do you have any more questions for Donna? Nathaniel said no and Jose proceeded with his closing. Donna, I have reviewed your work, attendance record, and grades. In all categories, you rate above average and excellent in attendance. Donna, Jose asked. "What category do you need improvement in to meet the criteria for being a team lead?"

"Mr. Gonzales," replied Donna.

"I need to improve my GPA. Mr. Gonzales no one in my family graduated from high school. Grades have never been important in my family. My brothers' got their GED, and they work in construction. I never had any reason to do well in school. We cannot afford college. After you started teaching the seminars I began to think about my grades, but it was too late. I am doing better in school and if I can get a B in my Spanish class I will have a B average."

"Donna, Sheltons will pay for a tutor for you. You can apply online for a grant for tutoring. They will pay the tutor directly. Sheltons has many benefits."

"Thank you, but I don't have a computer and I don't have time to go to the library after school."

"I will set up a computer in the employee breakroom, so the employees can use Sheltons benefit site."

Donna, you are an excellent employee. Nathaniel and I want to help you achieve your goal of being a part of the management team. Improve your grades and I see no reason you can't join our team and go to college."

"College, really Mr. Gonzales, do you think I could be accepted to a college?

"Yes, Donna, you could go to college" he replied.

Nathaniel, we don't have our next interview until 2:00 p.m. Let's talk about the interviews. What did you think?

"I learned a lot today about interviewing, setting goals, and encouragement. I had chalked Daniel up as a loser. Then you showed me that one day he may be a leader. If he does it will be because you believed in him instead of calling him a slacker."

"Nathaniel, every person has the potential to be great. Greatness must be nurtured and encouraged. I have reviewed your background to see how I can get you where you want to go in this company. May I make some suggestions? Jose asked.

"I'm open to your suggestions" replied Nathaniel. "Let me guess you have a chart" he laughed.

"Yes, I do. On it are your strengths, your weaknesses, and your goals. You have improved a great deal since I met you, Nathaniel. Your greatest attribute is that you know how to run the store and manage the crew. You get along with the customers although I would like to see you reach out to our customers as a whole more and our employees. For example, you will assist an elderly customer with their tray but not a young girl carrying a baby. You empathize with our adult employees when they don't come to work but don't with our young employees. There is resentment when you have to come in to cover a shift and it shows. I value you and Gretchen as

employees. I want both of you to run your stores. Nathaniel, you dropped out of college your junior year. I realize you have a wife and children, but Sheltons will pay for you to go back to school and let you work a reduced schedule with no cut in pay. If that is not in your plan I would like you to attend some management training seminars in our corporate offices. They will be invaluable to your training to become a general manager. You don't have to answer now. Talk it over with your family and tell me what you think. You can also work on your degree and attend the management development training seminars. You have my support no matter what you choose." Nathaniel thanked Jose. It was good to know that he valued him as an employee. He had some serious thinking to do. He would discuss the options with Beth.

Jose had some coffee and prepared for the last two interviews. One of these two men will be the new team leader. He was still on the fence between the two gentlemen. The applicant who got the position would depend solely on this interview.

Jose and Nathaniel sat down preparing for the interview. Jesus came back into his office. They both stood up and shook his hand.

Jose began asking the preliminary questions and then he got down to their real concerns. Jose your grades are on the borderline at this time. Your attendance record during the last six months has been poor to average.

The last six months' review was average. You have made some major changes in your attendance, performance, initiative, and

schoolwork.

What happened to make you change? My concern is that your new work ethic might change after you get the position. Can you tell me what happened?

Jesus thought about the question for a few minutes and began "When I applied for the position I had to measure myself against John. I was severely lacking. I had been tardy more times than on time. My grades were on the borderline. John started tutoring me in chemistry so that I could raise my GPA. I never thought about how my tardiness affected the other employees or the demands of the business. Mr. Gonzales, and Mr. Hendricks, I cannot afford to pay for college. I am an average basketball player. I spend most of my time on the bench. I want to go to college and major in business administration. I want a career with Sheltons. Through your seminars, you have shown me that I have to prepare a game plan for my life, make goals, and cross them off as I meet each of them. I have set up a chart of goals and my plan to obtain each goal. My goal is to become a team lead, graduate high school, attend college, and be a manager at Sheltons."

Jesus, how will you feel if you don't get the position?" asked Nathaniel.

"Mr. Hendricks, I will continue to work on my goals and try again next time.

"Jesus, do you have any questions of us?" asked Jose.

"No, I want to thank you both for the opportunity to interview

for the position."

Jose and Nathaniel sat down to discuss the interview.

Jose began "What a turnaround he has made in the last couple of months. I was impressed with his interview and his honesty. What are your thoughts, Nathaniel?

"I thought he was articulate and impressive. He is a viable candidate."

The last candidate would be John. They asked the preliminary questions and then Jesus addressed his concerns. John, you are an exceptional employee. You show initiative, you are excellent with the customers and the staff. Let me ask you this question? Where do you see yourself in five years?" asked Jose.

John thought about his answer.

"I see myself attending college on a basketball or academic scholarship studying engineering. I picture myself working over

the summer at IBM. I am currently in their mentorship program."
Nathaniel asked the obvious question.

"John, how does Sheltons" fit into your career plans?"

"I would like to continue to work at Sheltons while I am in high school
and the summer before I start college" replied John.

"John, being a team lead means taking on additional duties and
hours. If you had to choose between being a team lead and
sacrificing your mentorship with IBM or basketball which would
you choose?

John, before you answer think about it, and we will talk on
Monday.

"Thank you, Mr. Gonzales, and Mr. Hendricks, I will give it
some thought and discuss it with my family."

Nathaniel looked at Jose and smiled. He knew that John would
pick his mentorship and basketball. Given the same choice, Jesus
would pick becoming the new team lead. Jose would not make
the decision. John was the most qualified applicant. He would
decide his fate.

John went home and thought about the position and the
responsibilities of the new job. It would be challenging, and he
could handle it. He knew that being a manager at Sheltons was
not in his five-year plan. Basketball would give him a college
scholarship. His mentorship with IBM would give him
employment during the summer in his field of study. His

academic success would allow him to achieve a master's degree in engineering. He would turn down the position. Applying for the position gave him interviewing experience and helped him write down his plan and goals. Anything that kept him from achieving his goals would be eliminated.

He called Jose. He had made his decision.

"Jose, this is John Humphries. I've decided. I am choosing my mentorship and basketball. I would like to continue to work at Sheltons as a member of the team."

"John, I thought this would be your decision, and thank you for your honesty. I value you as an employee. You will receive a raise on your next paycheck. "

"Thank you Mr. Gonzales" replied John with excitement.

"Jesus, can I see you in my office?

Jesus went into Mr. Gonzales's office prepared for the worst.

"Jesus, we are proud to offer you the job of team lead. We were extremely impressed with your game plan and want to help you achieve it. You will be taking on additional tasks and scheduled for more hours on the weekend. Is there a conflict with basketball?

"No sir, I am ready to hang up my basketball uniform and work my plan."

Jose stood up and shook his hand. "Your new salary will be
……."

Jesus called his mom on his break. "Mom, I got the job. Now I begin my 5-year plan."

"Congratulations son, your father would be proud" exclaimed his mother.

Jesus had not heard from his father in a year. He wondered if he would be proud of him. After all, he was his bastard child.

CHAPTER 18

Tad came home disappointed. He had not accomplished his mission. Surprisingly, Donald was not surprised he had a daughter. He wondered if he knew all this time. He heard his message from Alicia and decided to meet with her. Maybe she had changed her mind. He would throw up his visit with Donald and see if she would bite. They set a lunch date for Thursday at 12:30 p.m.

Donald and Casey had talked all night. They decided to tell the twins they had a sister. Donald was ashamed of his secret but not of his daughter. They went into the twin's room together. Alison and Abigail immediately looked up when their parents came into the room.

Donald began, "You have a sister. Her name is Tammy Walker, and she lives in Oregon where her grandfather lives. She is 13 years old. Here is her picture."

"Why doesn't she live with us?" asked Alison.

"Another family adopted Tammy. I am her father, but she has a different mother" explained Donald.

"Alison began to cry. "Why was she adopted? Didn't you want her?

"Alison, I, and her mother were teenagers. She was adopted by wonderful people who love her very much."

Abigail asked, "Can she come live with us now?"

Donald answered. "No Abigail she has a wonderful home but maybe we can meet her. We are going to Salem this weekend to see Grandfather and maybe your sister."

Donald ordered a background check completed on Alicia and the Walkers. He was satisfied that the Walkers were excellent parents and that Alicia, and her husband were also. Now was the hard part, he made a call to Alicia.

"Hello, May I speak with Alicia." The voice sounded distantly familiar, but she couldn't place it.

"Alicia, it's Donald Cohen."

Alicia held her breath. Her nightmare had come true, and Tad had opened the door. Michael was watching his wife as tears formed in her eyes. He picked up the other line and listened. He started to hang up, but she gestured no to him. He remained on the line.

"Alicia, your brother came to see me. He told me about Tammy. Alicia, I knew in my heart that I had a child. I told my dad, but you left town. I am so sorry I hurt you. Thank you for having our child. Before I got married I told my wife. I knew one day this day would come. Please don't worry I will never try to take Tammy from her adoptive parents. I would like for my family to meet her. I have twin daughters Alison and Abigail. I have told them about Tammy. My fear is your brother. I don't know how far he will go to obtain custody for your family."

Alicia cried relieved that Tad's plan was cancelled. If they all formed a united front there was nothing he could do.

"Thank you, Donald. I have been so afraid."

"Alicia, I will be in town on Friday. I will be staying at my
dad's. Will you speak to the Walkers and see if they will let my
family meet her. My mom is deceased, but my dad would like to
meet her. I know that the Walkers will be reluctant for me to meet
her. I need to let my daughter know that I knew in my heart that
she was born, and I loved her.

Alicia took down his number. She could not promise anything,
but she did say she would ask. I will be in town by 1:30 p.m.
Please call me.

Michael pulled Alicia into his arms and held her. He understood
Donald's feelings. He knew how much he loved Christina. He
could not imagine having a child and not being able to see her.
He knew that Donald had caused her a lot of pain. They were
older now, both married and with families of their own. He
would not interfere. This was a decision that only
Alicia could make herself. The ultimate decision would be the
Walkers. They would be risking losing custody of Tammy a
second time, but could they deny a father his parental rights?

Alicia wanted to hurt him like he had hurt her, but God had
forgiven her. She could not judge Donald. They were both
young. He had matured. She would do what was best for her
daughter. She would not play God. She called the Walkers and

ask them to come over for lunch. They knew she had some news and agreed to meet with her at 2:00 p.m. They wanted to meet with Tad first.

Tad walked into the restaurant, sure of himself. He was going to

play his cards close to his heart. He was certain that Alicia would believe him. Even if he had not convinced Donald to re-open the adoption he had enough details to convince Alicia to file for custody. She would never let Donald get custody of Tammy. Alicia and Michael were at the table poised to hear his story.

They greeted him and then allowed him to speak.

"Alicia I took a trip to California to see Donald. To my surprise, he did not deny Tammy. He already knew and was making plans to seek custody. He is married with twin daughters and owns an accounting firm.

Tammy, I am afraid that he will take Tammy away from the Walkers.

It is best that you file for custody immediately."

"Tad, I spoke to Donald after your visit. He said he kicked you out of his office. He does not intend to pursue custody of Tammy. He does think that you are a lunatic and cannot be trusted. Tad, I do not want you near my daughter or my family. I hope you will drop this mission but if you do not you will never see my daughter again. We are leaving now."

Tad watched as Alicia and Michael walked out of his life. He had lost contact with the niece he never knew. What had he done? "Lord please forgive me.

Alicia and Michael approached the Walkers' house and rang the bell.

Tammy and Jonathan ran to the door hoping Christina was with

them.

Tammy hugged Alicia and Michael. Jonathan hung back waiting for his hug.

"Where's Christina?" Jonathan asked.

"She's at the ranch with my parents" replied Alicia.

Nancy heard them in the hallway talking and came to get them. She was anxious to hear what they had to say. Alicia told Nancy and John everything, including Tad's blotched trip to California. She loved her brother, but she could not allow him to destroy her relationship with her daughter. Alicia could see the fear on Nancy's face. She assured them that the decision to allow Donald to meet Tammy was theirs alone, but they would like to be present. John and Nancy held each other's hand. They looked at each other and said "This is Tammy's decision. We will let you know tomorrow."

Tammy, Jonathan, and their parents had a family meeting. They told Tammy that her biological father and his family wanted to meet her.

Tammy immediately stiffened. She remembered meeting Alicia and thinking she would take her away from her parents. "Where does my father live?" She looked at John and said you are my dad.

He hugged her. "He lives in California, is married, and has twin daughters, Alison, and Abigail.

Jonathan pouted, more girls. "Why doesn't anybody have a boy?"

"Would I have to go to California?" asked Tammy.

"No he and his family will be in town for the weekend." She looked at her brother remembering his reaction the first time.

"Jonathan" she asked. "Do you want to meet my father?"

"Can we meet him at the ranch?" Jonathan queried.

Tammy looked at her parents. "I think that can be arranged," said her mother.

Nancy made the telephone call to Alicia. Alicia called her parents to arrange for everyone to meet at the ranch.

Donald picked up the phone on the first ring. He thanked Alicia and asked for directions to the ranch. He hung up and hugged his wife. "We will meet our daughter on Saturday at Alicia's parents ranch." Casey felt a little uneasy. Was she ready to share Donald with his past? Her nightmare was now her reality.

CHAPTER 19

The preliminary trial would begin at 9:00 in courtroom 202.
Carl woke up early. His stomach was churning. He ran to the
bathroom and vomited. Mr. Summers had prepared him for the
worst. Today they would decide if there was enough evidence to
take their case to trial. Justin and Carl would be tried at the same
time.

The DA had offered a plea deal for two years for harassment and
intent to harm.

They would serve a year of the term if they had a year of good
behavior and a year's probation. He presented the deal to both
boy's attorney's and their parents knowing that they would
rather go to trial. He had done his research.

Dwight Summers and Blake Donavan had gone to college
together. They had roomed together during their sophomore year.
They had been on the debate team together. Dwight had gotten
suspended for a semester for his part in a fraternity pledge game
that put a student in the hospital. The injuries were not life-
threatening but both boys were suspended. Dwight returned to
school and graduated at the top of his class. Blake and Dwight
both made law review at the University of Michigan. Blake came
from money and defended money. Donavan had a diversity of
clients, but all could afford to pay his comparative fees. He
thought he knew Dwight's motivation. He suspected that Blake's
was the all mighty dollar, but he had his staff research every

aspect of this case. His staff had interviewed Glen Adams, Alan's best friend, his dad Dr. Tom Smith, Mrs. Bates, the school principal, and Robert Bates' parole officer. Due to the sensitivity of the matter, both attorneys agreed to interview the witnesses at one time. Moran knew their defense would be based on the fact that there were many contributing factors to Alan Bates's suicide and that the boy teasing was not the principal contributor.

Dwight and Blake had called a meeting of both families. They explained that both boys were being tried for the same crime. He thought that accessory to murder by suicide would be thrown out but verbal assault with the intent to harm and harassment would

be tried. They believed if they were tried by a jury that Alan's suicide would gain the empathy of the jury. The judge would only look at the facts. Could the DA prove without any doubt that it was their words that made Alan Bates pick up the gun and shoot himself? They wanted to try the case together.

Gladys wanted her case separate because she thought that Justin's hot shot attorney would blame everything on Carl. She did not trust him.

Ms. Blevins, "I understand your concern. I have known Blake since college. You trust me and I need you to trust him. I would never jeopardize the defense of my client. We are all in this together. The Houston's didn't think this Black attorney that would take a case paid for by the court was capable of defending their son.

Mr. Houston, first of all, that is a racist and classist statement. It also implies that you hired me because I have money and I am White. If I told you that Dwight's father was a Supreme Court judge and made lots of money would he be good enough to defend your son.? The only thing I will tell you is that I went to school with Dwight. He is a man of honor and integrity; He is not a legal aid attorney. He has been a criminal attorney for 20 years and has won more cases than I have. Is it his race that you don't like or the fact that he took this case for free."

"Mr. Donavan, I am not a racist. You can accuse me of wanting the best for my son. Maybe I should have hired him instead. His credentials suit me" said Mr. Houston. "I will agree to joint representation."

Both families met in Dwight's office to discuss the case. On Monday they would begin to prepare the boys for questioning. Blake had his private detective run a check on DA Moran. They wanted some idea as to his background and his personal life. There were some rumors that he was gay, but they had not been validated. He grew up in Kentucky. His father was a mine worker, and his mother was a teacher. He attended public school and received a scholarship to the University of Kentucky. He attended law school in Kentucky and took a job with legal aid. When the opportunity came to transfer to Oregon he took it. He started as an assistant DA and then was appointed district attorney when the DA retired before the end of his term. Since becoming district attorney he had a winning record, but he has not made a statement that was needed to win an election. This would be his test. It was a controversial case, and he must get a guilty verdict. The one thing they knew about Moran was that he was hungry, driven, and ambitious, but he was a man of integrity. He would come to court with a strong case and the burden of proof would be on their teams

They would put the probation officer, Alan Bates's mother, Robert Bates, and the principal on trial. They would prove without a doubt that neither Justin Houston nor Carl Blevins's statements were the smoking gun in Alan Bates's suicide. The attorneys presented their case to the judge. Judge Reinhart would interview each boy privately and ask them questions. The judge listened to the testimony of the principal, Alan Bates's mother, and the boys. He would render his decision tomorrow. The attorneys met with their clients. The judge will make his decision about the charges and the evidence. We are preparing for the worst. We will meet tomorrow afternoon to go over their testimony. We will take care of everything else. Judge Rinehart reviewed the testimony given by the mother, principal, and the boys. The boys had been coached to tell the truth but be evasive. They never admitted guilt. If lawyers were not involved he believed that the boys would have admitted their part, pled guilty to the lesser charges. They would have gotten time and mostly probation. The attorneys were retained to get an acquittal. This case would go to the jury. DA Moran had presented enough evidence to go to trial. The charges would be 1. malicious harassment, 2. causing bodily injury. These crimes carried a sentencing of one to five years.

The attorneys had asked for a charge of misdemeanor malicious harassment. He would only accept this charge if they pleaded guilty. These were serious charges. A young boy committed suicide. Only the jury could decide who was responsible. Dwight and Blake received the calls separately. They notified their clients. The trial would begin in two weeks.

CHAPTER 20

Mrs. Worthington came into the room to check on Stacey. She had gone to bed early last night. She wasn't feeling well. Since Stacy had contracted AIDS a common cold could become pneumonia or a major infection. She overreacted at the slightest scrape or accident. She waited for Stacy to come down the stairs, then she began to worry. She called her but she didn't answer. She called her again then ran up the stairs trying hard not to panic. She entered the room saw that the bathroom door was open and went in anticipating the worst. Stacey had passed out on the bathroom floor. She was sweating profusely. Her hair was matted. Her legs were limp. She checked her pulse. It was slow. She picked up the phone and called 911. She advised the ambulance that her daughter had AIDS and had passed out in the bathroom. She put a cold compress over her face, and she opened her eyes

 When I entered she was on the bathroom floor. She was sweating profusely. Her hair was matted. Her legs were limp. She checked her pulse. It was slow. She picked up the phone and called 911. She informed the operator that her daughter had AIDS and had passed out in the bathroom. She had put a cold compress on her eyes and opened her eyes. She felt relieved and asked her to try and stay awake. The ambulance arrived. She ran downstairs and led them upstairs. They quickly took her vitals and began an IV drip. They lifted her fragile body onto the stretcher and carried her downstairs. Mrs. Worthington called her husband and alerted him that they were on their way to the hospital. She rode in the ambulance with Stacey.

Stacey was wheeled into the emergency room for treatment. Mrs. Worthington waited in the hallway for her husband, Sam. Sam immediately ran through the door and began questioning his wife.

"What happened? She was okay yesterday. Did you check on her this morning? You realize that you went to bed early." Carolyn was reeling. Her daughter was in the hospital and her husband was hammering her with questions. She looked as if she was going to collapse herself. He saw her reaction and shut up. He pulled her into his arms for comfort.

"Carolyn I am sorry. I get so scared when something happens to Stacey. I did not mean for you to think that I was blaming you. I love you. Can you tell me what happened?"

"I got up and fixed breakfast. Stacey usually gets up puts on her clothes, and comes down to eat with me. I waited for her to come down, and when she didn't I waited for a few minutes then called her. I thought. maybe she was in the bathroom, so I called her again. When she didn't respond I ran upstairs to get her. When I entered the room the bathroom door was open. I got there as soon as I could. When I reached the bathroom entrance she was lying on the bathroom floor. I should have gone sooner. I'm so sorry."

"Carolyn, replied Sam. We can't watch Stacey 24/7 but there are some precautions we need to take so that she can contact us if anything is wrong. I am going to call the AIDS Foundation and get some advice on an alert system that we can install so that

Stacey can alert us when she's in trouble. Carolyn could not put her finger on what caused this crisis. They had gone out to eat last night and after eating Stacey felt nauseated and tired. She went to bed. Stacey had a hamburger with tomato and lettuce and some fries. Caroline and Joe had fish. They felt fine.

The nurse came out to get the Worthington's. She said that Stacey had salmonellosis, commonly known as food poisoning. They questioned her about her menu last night. They told her she had a medium rare hamburger with tomato and lettuce. There were no leftovers. Food poisoning could occur if the meat is left out or from the tomato. They would treat Stacey's illness, by infusing liquids through her IV. Because she has AIDS they needed to get her T-cell count back to normal and make sure they treated the food poisoning.

Mr. and Mrs. Worthington,

"We are moving Stacey into a room for tonight so that we can monitor her treatment. You can sit with her until we have a room ready

Mr. and Mrs. Worthington went in to see their daughter. They each pulled up a chair. Stacey looked at them and smiled.

"I did it again. I was trying to get to the bathroom. I felt myself falling but by then it was too late. My stomach was hurting, and I was all clammy. I had diarrhea. I didn't know whether to throw up or get to the bathroom. Unfortunately, I passed out before I could do either one. I knew you would panic when I didn't come down and come get me. Thank you for panicking.
I love you. When can I go home?"
"You will have to stay overnight so that they can monitor your symptoms.
They are going to move you into a room. If your t-cell count is okay tomorrow you can go home" replied her dad.
"Stacey we are going to set up some safeguards in your room and downstairs so if you are in trouble you can always reach us. This wasn't life threatening, but it could have been. Your mother is going to stay the night with you tonight and I will be back in the morning. I will stay with you until you are ready to go to sleep."
Stacey hugged her parents. They thanked God she would be all right.

Stacey went home the next day. They began the installation of an alert system on Thursday. They could not protect her from her illness, but they could make sure they would be able to respond quickly if she were in danger. Time was not on her side. This system could save her life.

CHAPTER 21

Today was a good day. Rita was coming home. Rita had been in the hospital for two weeks. The second week while they were monitoring her symptoms she had a tutor come from the sickle cell foundation to help her catch up on her missed assignments. The tutors had been invaluable in helping Rita keep her grades up even though she was in the hospital. Although Rita was in a coma she was still able to hear everything that had been said. John had said some pretty sweet things, and she loved him. Tommy was right. The two of them were soul mates. One day they would be able to date. For now they would remain good friends. Tommy wasn't like other boys. He was smart and easy to talk to. He was interested in her life, and he allowed her to share his secret thoughts. He treated her as an equal. In two more years they would be able to go to the movies or maybe a skating party together. It was at these times that she thought about her disease and her mortality. She wanted to live long enough to get married, become a research scientist and have children. She believed she could do all of this. By the grace of God she would.

John, Henry, and her mother came into the hospital room.

"Rita "John yelled. "Are you ready to blow this joint?"

"I certainly am. Let's go. I don't even mind riding in the wheelchair."

"We have to wait for the discharge nurse, "said her mom. " Then we'll be ready to go. Henry why don't you and John take Rita's things down and bring the car around. I'll get Kathy to bring the paperwork and we will be out of here in a few minutes."

Henry gave his daughter a hug. John and he took the bags downstairs.

Rita looked at her mother and asked.

"Do you think I will be able to go to college, get married and have children one day?"

"I absolutely do Rita" replied her mother. I don't have a crystal ball, but I see a bright future for you. We must never take life for granted. New drugs and treatments will help you live longer but you have to maintain your GPA, and be open to all the possibilities that life has to offer. Life is a journey. It's not always easy but you can never give up on yourself or your future. I love you. We are always here for you."

"I love you to" exclaimed Rita.

The nurse came in to sign the discharge papers and rolled Rita down to the front exit. There was her father waiting patiently at the car for them to arrive.

"Rita do you feel like getting something to eat or would you rather get some rest and eat at home" her dad asked.

"Are you kidding I want to go out and get the biggest hamburger I can eat."

Everyone laughed. Off to Sheltons they went.

John was scheduled to work this afternoon, so he had brought his

clothes in the car with him. He had gotten a raise on his last
check. He continued his excellent work ethic. He could see that

Jesus was becoming a good team lead. He was glad he got the
job. Basketball season would start in the fall, and he would cut
his hours back. Jesus had decided to quit basketball in order to
focus on his grades and his new position. They were both happy
with their choices.

Jesus was never told but he knew that John had turned the job
down. Now he had to prove to everyone including himself that
he deserved the position. His mom was so proud of him. She said
he was finally becoming a man. His mom had finally started
dating. It was good for her. Sometimes he felt like she was
neglecting him, but he knew that was selfish. He knew she loved
him.

John went to the counter and ordered their meal. He told them he
would pay today. He used his company family discount and
brought back orders for everyone. Jose came out and greeted the
family.

"Rita, I'm so glad to see you are out of the hospital" said Jose.
"More than one of my employees was concerned about you. On
that note it is time for Tommy to go on break. I'm sure he wants
to see you. He'll thank me by working extra hard when he
gets back on the clock."

Rita smiled. Jose went back to the kitchen and a few minutes later Tommy was sitting at their table.

"Hey Mr. and Mrs. Humphries. Rita I didn't realize that you were getting out today. I would have told Debbie, and we would have come over to see you."

"I'm sure mom will make me rest tonight but I hope everyone will come by tomorrow after church. I'm supposed to sing a solo tomorrow. I hope they didn't give my solo to somebody else."

"Rita, Mrs. Dunlap called, and I told her you would be home this Sunday and would be able to sing" said her mother.

"Rita, we'll see you at church tomorrow. Rita, can you sing? I don't want anybody throwing tomatoes."

Tommy laughed. "You know I'm just teasing."

"Tommy how is your mother?" asked Rita.

He stopped and looked at her. After all she had been through she still took the time to ask about his mother. One day Rita would be his wife. He just knew it.

"She's home recuperating. She will have to go back for reconstructive surgery but right now she is taking out patient radiation then she will begin chemotherapy. My dad has been both a blessing and a nuisance. He is starting to get on our nerves. Hopefully, he will be returning to the office soon."

"Your dad working at home, what else happened while I was out of circulation. We'll catch up with everyone tomorrow."

Jose came out to the table. "John, Jackie just called in for tonight. I know you are with your family, but can you clock in a little early today. I would appreciate it."

"Mr. Gonzales, Let me get my clothes out of the car and I'll be on the floor in a few minutes" replied John.

John hugged his sister and exited to the car.

"Rita, Henry let's go. I don't want to wear her out her first night

home" said her mother.

Mary had slept at the hospital for the last two weeks. She was as excited as Rita to be home, back in her bed, in her husband's arms.

Nathaniel came in early. He knew that Jackie had called out and he was prepared to cover until John came in to work. Jose met him as he was getting ready to help on front line. John is going to clock in early, so we have time to talk for a minute. He waited for John to take the front register and walked into his office.

"Nathaniel, have you thought about your future here at Sheltons and what you would like to do toward meeting your goals" asked Jose.

"I was going to meet with you tomorrow to discuss my options. I mapped out my action plan. I would like to reduce my schedule to forty hours and take online classes to finish my degree. I called the university, and I can enroll this summer. I will need twenty four credit hours to obtain my degree in business administration. After I complete my degree I would like to begin taking classes at the management development center at corporate. After your interviews I looked at all the benefits available to management and I was astonished. Do you think this plan is feasible considering the demands of our business?" asked Nathaniel.

"Nathaniel, when you enroll in classes let me know and I will hire a part-time manager to work the additional hours. Once you register I will sign off on your paperwork and reduced schedule. Sheltons will pay your tuition directly to the school. They will continue to pay as long as you maintain a B average. If you don't you will have to foot the bill yourself, but it can be deducted out of your paycheck monthly.

You will maintain your current salary while you are in school contingent upon your grades. I know you have a family. This is an opportunity that you must take seriously. I will give you all the support that I can. When you finish your degree you will get a raise in pay. At that time you can begin to register for the management development training given by corporate office. These classes will prepare you for General, District and Area Manger. We will meet every 3 months to go over your action plan. I will also be meeting with Gretchen to go over her action plan."

Nathaniel left Jose's office smiling. He was a new man with a plan.

Rita was glad to sleep in her own bed. She went straight to sleep after she said her prayers. Mary couldn't help checking on her frequently. Her little girl was home.

Bill picked up Tommy and John from work. Bill dropped John off at the house. Tommy turned to his father and asked him "Can we go to church tomorrow? Rita is singing a solo."

"Yes, we can. Can you set the alarm and get the kids up. Betsy is off tomorrow" asked his dad.

"I got this," joked Tommy.

The Colbert family got dressed. They were eating breakfast when Toni came downstairs dressed for church. She looked at her family and smiled. We have much to be thankful for.

Bill got up kissed his wife and pulled out her chair at the table.

The Worthington's were busily getting dressed for Sunday

services. As usual, Stacey was still trying to find something to wear. The children would be singing today so she had to wear a khaki skirt and a white blouse but which skirt and what blouse, decisions, decisions.

Rita woke up early to practice her solo. She knew she would be lifting her voice in praise to God. Everything would be ok.

"Rita, Let's go before we're late.

After the Lord's Prayer Rita walked to the mike and began her solo "Why do I feel discouraged... .....His eye is on the sparrow. I know he's watching over me.

Mary and Toni made a few phone calls after church, and they all

met at the Colbert's. Bill called Jason's' Deli' and had them
bring some sandwich trays, fruit, and desserts. Henry picked up
some buckets of chicken, potato salad, and baked beans. The
Walkers brought some plates, drinks, and macaroni and cheese.
The McKnight's brought green bean casserole. The
Worthington's and the Hayden's brought dessert. The
Hernandez family brought some black beans and rice. Dr. Smith,
Ellen, and Glen brought salad.

All the families were together just like in old times. Toni was

tired but she knew how blessed she was to be able to share this
time with her extended family.

"Hey," Mr. McKnight yelled out.

"Let's play baseball.

Everyone gathered their gloves and hit the field. It was the dad's
against the kids. Mr. Hernandez had been practicing at the
baseball arcade. He wanted to make his son proud.

Mr. Hernandez came to the plate. Abele held her breath as her
husband struck at the ball.

"Strike 1" yelled the ump.

"Strike 2" yelled the ump.

Alfredo focused as the ball was thrown to him. He took a fast
swing at the ball. You could hear the thump as the bat connected
with the ball. Alfredo smiled as he strode around the bases as the
ball seemed to fly over the fence. He looked at his son and threw

his hand in the air as he crossed home plate.

CHAPTER 22

"All rise the honorable Judge Rinehart is present" projected the bailiff. "You may be seated."

Judge Rinehart began with instructions. "This is a closed case. No one is to speak to the press or any other source regarding this case. The state may begin with its opening statement.

The case presented before is quite simple. Alan Bates was a boy with his demons. He was a victim of sexual molestation. Despite this, he worked to get out of the remedial class. He found help and support from his friend's stepfather, Dr. Smith. He was tutored until he was promoted to the 3^{4th} grade.

Justin Houston and Carl Blevins with malicious intent teased Alan and harassed him to the point of no return. He killed his father and later after being taunted again he put the gun to his head and pulled the trigger. It was the actions of these two boys that caused Alan Bates to commit suicide."

The jury looked at the two boys' faces. Carl had tears in his eyes. Justin would not make eye contact.

Donavan Blake opened the case for the boys. "Something tragic happened on April 25, 2010, Alan Bates committed suicide. The state will provide evidence that these two boys teased and harassed this young man. We will prove that other factors contributed to Alan's suicide. We will show that Alan was an angry child. His father molested him. His mother failed to protect him. His school put him in harm's way by not enforcing the bullying law. The question is not if the boys contributed to this incident but whether they were the smoking gun that made Alan Bates pull the trigger. Only you can be the judge.

The state calls Justin Houston to the stand. Justin was sworn in and ready to testify.

Moran asked for permission to approach the bench.

"Justin, tell the court how you knew Alan Bates."

"I didn't know him. He used to be in the slow class, but he was in regular classes now."

"Justin, how did you find out about Alan's father?"

"We were surfing the web for sex offenders. We thought it would be fun to see if there were any in our area. When we reduced the search we saw Alan's father. We had heard rumors a long time ago. We put two and two together."

"Justin, you said you had heard rumors earlier. Did anyone confront Alan or tease him when the rumors were being heard?"

"No, not really, Not that I remember."

"What did you do with your evidence against his father?"

"We confronted him in the cafeteria. Carl yelled something at him. The only thing I asked him, was if his friend Glen was his boyfriend."

"What was his reaction to what you and Carl said." "He ran out of the lunchroom and out the door crying."

"What was your reaction? Did you feel bad, did you smile, just exactly how did you react?"

"I got my lunch until they took me to the office and put us in detention.

"When did you see Alan again?"

"The principal had called us to the office. We were being suspended. We went to get our books and we ran into Alan.

"How did you react when you saw him walking down the hall? After all, you believed it was his fault that you got suspended. What did you say to him?"

"I called him a pervert and blamed him for getting me suspended from school. I told him maybe we ought to, but his voice got lower and lower."

"Justin, I need you to repeat your answer to the court."

"I said maybe we ought to give it to him in the butt like his father did."

"What happened next?"

"He pulled a gun out of his pocket and then we heard a loud noise. Then he fell to the floor and there was blood everywhere." Justin's mind went back to that tragic day. He kept rambling. I felt water flowing down my leg, then someone took me away to the office."

"I am finished with this witness" relinquished Moran.

Donavan Blake walked toward his client and began the questioning.

"Justin, why did you confront Alan in the cafeteria?" he asked.

"We were just fooling around."

"Justin, when you were teasing Alan did you think he would hurt himself?"

"No, we knew it would bother him, but we never thought he would kill himself."

"Justin, why did you confront Alan the day of the shooting?

"We got suspended and I didn't think it was fair. I was angry at him because I was going to get in trouble when I got home."

"Justin, did you mean for Alan to kill himself?"

'No, Justin said as tears came to his eyes"

That's all I have your honor.

"Mr. Moran, do you want to redirect?" asked Judge Rinehart.

"Yes your honor, may I approach."

"Justin, you testified you were just fooling around. Did you ever give one thought to the consequences of your actions?

"No sir" Jason replied in a murmur.

"Jason I have one last question. Think carefully before you speak. Was it your intent to hurt Alan with your words?" Justin began to cry. As he began to answer the question his attorney shook his head no. Justin answered the question. "I plead the fifth."

Judge Rinehart turned to Justin.

"You may be seated, Justin."

Carl took the stand.

Moran came close to ask questions of Carl.

"Carl, why did you confront Alan in the cafeteria?" asked Moran.

"We wanted to tease him about his father."

"What did you say to Alan in the cafeteria?"

"I yelled at him and said that we heard his father was a pervert. I asked him if he got out of the remedial class by giving sexual favors" replied Carl.

"Carl, why did you try to hurt Alan?"

"Justin is my only friend. I thought, if I had information on Alan the kids would look up to me and want to hang around me. I thought it would make me more popular."

"Carl, do you get popular at school for teasing other kids?"

"Yes, the teachers even overlook them sometimes."

"What did you say to Alan the day of his death?" inquired Moran.

"Nothing, the next thing I heard was the gunshot, replied Carl."

"Carl, how did you feel when you saw Alan's body fall to the ground?" "I felt guilty, sick, nauseated. I wanted to die with him."

Dwight Summers began his questioning.

"Carl, we cannot turn back the hands of time. Do you regret your actions?"

"I wish I had never hurt him. He looked at Mrs. Bates. "I am so sorry. I didn't mean it. I'm so sorry.

DA Moran declined to cross-examine.

"We will adjourn until tomorrow until Monday at 9:00 a.m.

Dwight hugged Carl. "You did a good job."

His mother hugged him. They left the courtroom to go home. It would be a long weekend.

Justin's mom came over and hugged her son. "Let's get some ice cream and try to enjoy the weekend. I am taking the weekend off so we can spend some time together."

They walked out together hand in hand. Justin could not believe his mother had hugged him. She never showed affection. Sarah did not want to waste any more time, afraid of losing her son. She wanted her son to know that she loved him.

CHAPTER 23

Tammy woke up early. She was excited and scared to meet her dad. Would he love her like Alicia did? Alicia and Michael were good to her. She knew that Alicia loved her, but the Walkers were her family. This is where she wanted to stay. Christina was her baby sister and Jonathan was her little brother. She was happy. She had lots of friends. Two of her friends had been in the hospital, and Stacey and Rita were home. They had a cookout last Sunday. It was good to see everyone in Plains Estates.

Alicia was nervous. She thought back to the confrontation between her and Donald so long ago. She met him outside to tell him she was pregnant. He laughed in her face. He told her she wasn't pinning a pregnancy on him. There was no way he was the father. He didn't know how many boys she had slept with before him. She ran home crying. He was her first and they had only had sex twice. How could he think that of her? She went straight to her room and cried all night. She eventually told her parents. There was a lot of screaming praying and crying. She refused to tell them the father's name. She was afraid they would confront him. It was hard enough that he had rejected her and the baby. She didn't want to be embarrassed in front of her family. Now she would come face to face with him, his wife, and their twin daughters. She would face her accuser. She had found happiness with her husband and her two daughters. A part of her was happy for Donald but a little part of her didn't think he deserved to see Tammy after abandoning her.

This was not about her. It was about her daughter feeling complete. She heard Christina crying and went to get her out of bed. Today would be an interesting day.

Donald got the children up and let Casey sleep. He knew she was on edge about meeting Alicia and their daughter. He tried to assure her that Alicia had her own life now, was married, and had a daughter. Even if Alicia were single they were never a couple. They had sex a couple of times. He was surprised she would even speak with him after all the mean things he said to her. He looked his wife eye to eye and held her. I love you. I need to meet my daughter. I need to redeem my sins of the past.

Nancy went downstairs and started breakfast. It was a two-hour ride to the ranch. She had the waffle iron heated and ready. She was beginning to mix the batter when Tammy came into the room.

"Can I help?" she asked.

"Can you wash the blueberries and put a bowl of them in the batter for me?

Tammy washed the blueberries and poured the bowl in the batter. She watched intently as her mother added the other ingredients.

"Tammy, can you crack eight eggs for me and start to mix them" her mother asked.

Tammy reached for the eggs. Her father walked up behind her.

"Let me get the eggs for you. Tammy." He spoke. "I want one of my famous western omelets. What do you say Tammy? Are you game?"

"If she's not I sure am" yelled Jonathan. "I want bacon with mine.

John took out the vegetables and sliced them. Tammy mixed the eggs and milk, while Jonathan added the seasoning. Nancy prepared the waffles. While Dad fixed the omelets Tammy and Jonathan poured the orange juice and set the table. The coffee pot beeped, and they knew that breakfast was ready.

They sat down at the table and held hands. Tammy led the family in prayer.

"Dear God. We thank you for my amazing family. Thank my mom and dad for not being afraid to share my love with my biological parents. Bless us today and our extended family. Amen."

After breakfast, everyone chipped in and cleaned the kitchen. They all got dressed for the trip to the ranch. They packed some snacks and got on the road.

The Steele's were ready to go early. They wanted to help her mother prepare for the guests to arrive. They packed the car and got on the road.

Donald and his father had prepared breakfast for everyone. Donald talked to his father about his fears.

"Dad, I have a daughter that I have never met. What if she is afraid of me? What if she will never love me? I am blessed. I

have Casey and the girls. I need for my daughter to forgive me. I need her to want me in her life. I will never do anything to hurt Alicia or Tammy again. I love you, dad. You have been there since day one when Alicia told me that she was pregnant. You have been there for me over the years. You understand the emptiness and my pain better than anyone. You have cried with me over the loss of my child. You will finally meet your granddaughter. We have been blessed."

Donald went upstairs to talk with his daughters. He sat on the bed with the two of them.

"Abigail and Alison we are going to the ranch to meet your sister. Thank you for welcoming her into the family. Your mommy and I love you and your sister very much. Daddy's heart hurt because he had a child that he did not

know. A part of me was missing. Now I know all my girls and I am blessed."

He hugged his daughters and kissed them on the cheek.

"Daddy, Abigail asked. Can we go now?"

"We're ready to go" agreed Alison.

Tad paced the floor upset with his self. The family was meeting at the ranch.

Donald and his family, The Walkers and their family, Alicia, Ted, and his parents were all meeting at the ranch. He was the villain, but he had brought Tammy and her biological family together. He had time to think about his actions since even his

wife was angry with him. How would he feel if somebody tried to take his girls away from him? It would devastate him.

He understood why everyone was so angry with him. In time they would understand and forgive him. God help me.

Alicia, Michael, and Christina arrived first.

"Mom, thank you for letting the family get together," said Alicia.

"Alicia, I'm still angry with Donald but I will let go for Tammy."

Shortly afterward The Walkers arrived. The children went to play by the stables. A car pulled into the drive right behind Ted. Donald got out of the car. What a difference a few years make thought Alicia. Michael and Alicia went out to meet Donald and his wife. Donald opened the door and freed the girls from their car seats. They were beautiful little girls. The girls went to stand by their father. Another person got out of the car. He was an older gentleman. Alicia assumed it was Donald's father. Michael stuck out his hand.

"Donald, I am Alicia's husband Michael." He extended his hand to Casey and the girls. Alicia stood beside her husband. Donald noted that she had grown up to be a beautiful woman. He shook her hand.

Abigail yelled out. "Where is our sister? We want to meet her." Everyone laughed. Abigail had broken the ice.

Alicia looked from one to another. "I'm Abigail. Alison has the yellow barrettes."

"Okay, Abigail let's go inside." They grabbed their father's hand, and they all went inside. Alicia made the introductions. Her mother suggested they all go into the other room to talk. Casey and Mr. Cohen stayed with the twins.

"Donald I need to know your intentions toward our daughter?" asked Nancy.

"That is a fair question, replied Donald. When Alicia told me she was pregnant I rejected her. I knew she was a virgin and that the baby was mine. I panicked. Several days later I told my dad. He wanted me to do the right thing. He looked at Alicia. I went to your house, and you had moved away. I knew in my heart that I had a child, and I loved that child. I told my wife before we married. I have prepared for this moment since I was 15. I only want to meet and know my daughter. I will never seek custody. Please do not be afraid."

"I appreciate your honesty, Donald. I want Tammy to have some time alone with you before she meets the family. I will go get her." spoke John.

Donald was visibly nervous. Tammy came into the room. She

looked at her parents. They smiled and hugged her. Then she looked at Donald. She stared for a minute looking for his features in her. She had his lips. She now knew where she came from. Surprisingly, her father was Jewish.

Alicia said they were going to leave so Donald could have some time with Tammy.

Donald knelt in front of his daughter. He asked her permission to hug her. "I have loved you all of your life. I hoped that I would one day meet you. I am sorry I was not man enough to be a father to you when you were born. Please forgive me."

"Donald I forgive you. When she called him by his first name his heart sank. He had always envisioned that when they met there would be this instantaneous bond. She would call him daddy, and all would be forgiven. He knew it would take time, but he was willing to wait for as long as it took. I am happy with my parents. They are the best parents in the world. I have a

brother Jonathan that I want you to meet.

I want to meet my sisters and your wife. Jonathan wants a

brother. Alicia said not now so I hope you will have a boy so

Jonathan can have a brother."

Donald hugged his daughter, then she went to get Jonathan.

Donald went to get his daughters, his father, and his wife. They

all came in at the same time.

Tammy met her sisters Abigail and Alison. Everyone met

143

Jonathan. Casey welcomed Tammy and Jonathan into the family. Jonathan said as Tammy warned.

"Are you guys going to have a son? I could use a brother. I don't care which family has one."

They all laughed. The Walkers had already met the rest of the family.

"Tammy asked Donald. "Who is the older man?"

"Tammy, meet your Abrham Benjamin Cohen."

"Hi grandfather, I don't have two of you."

"Good, Jonathan, may I be your grandfather too?"

"Definitely," Jonathan responded.

Everyone gathered in the dining room. Mrs. Adams said grace and lunch was served. It had been a good day. Tammy now knew her biological parents. She had an extended family. The most important thing was that she would stay where she belonged. She would remain with the Walkers.

Alicia walked hand in hand with Michael. She told him "I was prepared to hate him but then I realized we were too young to be parents. God blessed Tammy with a wonderful family. He blessed both of us with being able to not only see our daughter but be able to share in her life. Tad had a mission. It was misdirected but it brought three families together. God had a mission and he used Tad to make it happen. She would talk to Tad but not right now. He needed to suffer a little bit.

Donald stayed up late talking to his father. He would come home often so that the twins could get to know their sister and they could know their daughter. He was content. He wanted more. He wanted her to call him daddy but for now, it was enough. He kissed his daughters good night and went to bed.

CHAPTER 24

"All rise the honorable......

"You may call your first witness," said Judge Rinehart.

The state calls Mrs. Bates.

Mrs. Bates was sworn in under oath.

"Mrs. Bates," asked DA Moran. After the two defendants confronted Alan in the cafeteria what happened?

"I got a call from the principal. He said that two boys were teasing Alan at school, and he had run away."

"Did you see your son again Mrs. Bates?"

"No, the last time I saw my son was when he left for school that morning."

"What happened after your son ran away."

"I received a telephone call from the police they said that my husband had been shot and they were looking for Alan."

"What happened next?" inquired DA Moran.

"The next message I got was that my son was dead. He had committed suicide."

She could barely speak between sobs.

DA Moran stopped and then asked her one last question.

"Mrs. Bates, Do you believe that your son would still be alive if the defendants had not teased and humiliated him?"

"Yes, I do," said Mrs. Bates

"Your honor we reserve the right to question this witness later," said Mr. Summers.

"Sir, the state rest," said DA Moran.

"You may call your first witness" said Judge Rinehart.

"Your honor we call Mr. Bernard Gibson to the stand."

Blake began the questioning.

"Mr. Gibson," he asked. "How did you know Robert Bates?"

"I was his parole officer."

"How was the relationship between Alan Bates and his father?"

"It was strained. Alan hated his father"

"Did you find Mr. Bates remorseful for his actions?"

"He refused to apologize to his son. I told him it would help his son heal but he could not face his hurt. He had been molested by his father."

"Mr. Gibson, in your opinion did Robert Bates contribute to his son's suicide?"

Mr. Gibson answered quickly "Yes"

DA Moran came close to the witness stand and began questioning the witness.

"Mr. Gibson, are you a psychiatrist?"

"No"

"Are you a licensed psychologist?

"No"

"So your assumptions are based on your educated opinion as a parole officer. Is that correct?"

"Yes"

"I don't have any more questions, your honor."

Dwight Simmons stood up to redirect.

"Mr. Gibson, did you speak with Mr. Bates about his relationship with his son?"

"Yes"

"So your opinion is based not on conjecture but on your interaction with Mr. Bates. Is that correct?"

"My opinion is based on my interaction with Mr. Bates and 20 years of experience working with sex offenders."

"You may step down. Mr. Gibson"

We call Sebastian Kline to the stand.

"Mr. Kline, can you tell us your position at Glendale Elementary?"

"I am the school principal."

Mr. Kline, did you know Alan Bates well."

"Alan was a nice young boy. He had personal problems and had seen the guidance counselor many times."

"Mr. Klein, was Alan a good student?"

"Alan's issues had affected his grades, and he was put in the remedial class last year."

"Mr. Kline, did any other children tease Alan because he was in the remedial class?"

"Children are mean and cruel. Children tease other children. We punish the more serious cases. That is all we can do."

'Mr. Kline, in your opinion, was Alan's suicide a result of the teasing over the last year or two confrontations in his life."

"I believe it was an accumulation of the tragedies in his life."

Moran got up to cross.

"Mr. Kline, I only have a couple of questions. Was Alan improving in school?"

"Yes, he had gotten out of the remedial class."

"In your opinion, as a PhD in psychology would Alan Bates be alive today if these two boys had not taunted him?"

"Yes, in my opinion, he would be emotionally battered but alive."

We call Janice Bates to the stand. Your honor Mrs. Bates will be listed as a hostile witness.

Blake would break Mrs. Bates. It was the only way to save these two boys from 5 years in a juvenile detention center.

Blake began the questioning.

Mrs. Bates, why did you divorce your husband?"

One day I came home from work and found my husband in the bathroom while my son was in the bathtub. He was touching himself and my son. I put him out and filed for divorce."

"Mrs. Bates, when you filed for divorce did you press charges against your husband for sexual abuse?"

"No, he threatened to take my children. I was a housekeeper."

"Mrs. Bates, did you fight Mr. Bates for full custody of the

149

children?"

"No"

"Mrs. Bates, did your husband have visitation with the children?"

"Yes"

"Mrs. Bates, did you know that your husband was still molesting your son?"

"No, Every time Alan came home I would question him, and he would say nothing bad happened."

"Mrs. Bates isn't it true that it took an outsider to turn in your husband. Isn't it true that you didn't protect your own son from harm?"

Mrs. Bates started crying.

Blake paused to let Mrs. Bates compose herself then he went in for the kill.

"Mrs. Blake isn't it true that the root cause of your son's suicide was not the taunting of my clients but the molestation by your husband and the failure by you to protect him from harm.

Mrs. Bates sobbed "I did the best I could. I didn't want to lose my children. I didn't molest my son; I didn't taunt him. I tried to protect him from the cruelty of others. I did the best I could. I did not want him to pay for the sins of his father."

Blake stepped back. He had done what he had to do to protect his client. At this moment he hated himself.

"Your honor we rest our case."

Dwight took Blake's place. They had discussed their strategy. There was no way that a Black man could attack a white woman in court. They knew that Blake would be the one to question her and he would show no mercy.

"Tomorrow I will hear closing arguments" said Judge Rinehart.

Dwight and Blake stayed up for hours preparing their closing statement.

Dwight Simmons would close for the two boys. He was an experienced criminal attorney. He had to get the jury to have reasonable doubt. He believed they had showed the jury that there were many factors that led to Alan Bates suicide. The question was did they prove that the boys were not one of these factors. Dwight prepared his speech and Blake listened.

Janice held her daughter close to her and cradled Christina in her arms.

She sang softly. God please protect my daughter from harm. It will be over soon, and we will leave this life behind. She would take the life insurance and open a bakery. She would never trust someone else to protect her child. She had changed. Their life would be better.

Mrs. Houston tucked her son into bed. Justin I love you. Before you were born I had three miscarriages. I lost three children before they were born. I lived afraid to love you. I was afraid I would lose you. I'm sorry that I didn't tell you this before now. I understand Mrs. Bates guilt because I feel like I let you down so much that you took your hurt out on an innocent boy. May God forgive both of us?

Carl got down on his knees to pray to God. He looked at his

mother.

"Mom, will you pray with me?" he asked. "You don't have to say anything I will pray for us."

Mrs. Blevins kneeled down to pray with her son. She bowed her head and closed her eyes. She would respect her son's wishes.

CHAPTER 25

Mrs. McKnight picked up Toni Colbert and Debbie first. They were going on an outing. Next, they picked up Rita and Mary and Stacey and Mrs. Worthington. Jennifer had called the back window. The last group to be picked up was Tammy and Nancy Walker. Today was a mother-daughter spa day. They wanted to get out and enjoy themselves. They went to the spa and had pedicures and manicures. The women had facials. They all finished in the salon. The girls had their hair washed and curled while the ladies enjoyed haircuts and make-up.

After they finished they decided to go to lunch before going shopping.

They decided on a restaurant close by that had burgers and salads.

They all ordered their food and were having a great time. Toni was happy, but glad they were taking breaks between events. They were going to take the girls to the children's ballet.

"Come on girls we don't want to be late for the ballet. If we get out in time we will have time to shop" said Jan McKnight."

They all got into the van and off she drove. The ballet was Swan Lake. The girls loved the ballet. Mrs. Colbert and Mary Humphries had seen it several times, so they took the time to catch up.

"Mary how is Rita doing?" asked Toni.

"Rita is getting stronger every day" replied Mary "I hear Bill is working at home. How's that working for you?"

"I love my husband. I took my last chemo treatment so he will go back to work next week. I can't wait" she laughed excitedly."

Jan and Carolyn came to join them.

"I thought we would go shopping" questioned Carolyn. "Are you up to it Toni?"

"I'll be okay as long as I have a mommy chair," said Toni

The ballet was over and the girls were ready to go shopping. Jan rode down to the Mall. They had a good afternoon of shopping then stopped at Baskin Robbins and enjoyed some ice cream. The girls went into one more shop to look around.

Afterward, they would be ready to leave. The ladies had some downtime. They sipped on iced tea and caught up on the gossip. It had been a long day, and everyone was tired. The girls were quiet in the back seat. Mary and Carolyn were chatting quietly. Toni was nodding in the front seat. Jan stopped at the stop sign before turning into the neighborhood.

Jan looked both ways and began to drive. Out of nowhere came a car crashing into the front of them. The car seemed to have a life of its own, crashing into another car. Jan fell forth on the steering wheel. She heard someone say call 911.

The paramedics and the fire truck came. They pulled a body from the wreckage and pronounced her dead.

CHAPTER 26

"All rise....

The state would begin its opening summation.

DA Moran began. "Alan Bates is dead. He committed suicide. The question is whether these two boys with their malicious taunting led Alan Bates to take his own life. The boys themselves have admitted to the taunting. The principal testified that they only punished severe cases of taunting. Carl Blevins and Justin Houston were suspended for their actions. Justin and Carl with the intent of seeking revenge confronted Alan Bates and led him to not only kill his father but take his own life. We cannot bring this child back to life, but we can bring him justice from his persecutors.

Dwight stood before the jury. If the only issue were malicious taunting my clients would be guilty. They teased Alan Bates. Alan Bates was an emotionally battered young man. He was a victim of his father's abuse.

He hated his father for his actions. He couldn't seem to escape his past.

He tried to turn his life around, but his father was released from jail. He felt like there was no way out from the pain except to take his life. Carl Blevins and Justin Blake did not make Alan Bates put the gun to his head and pull the trigger. It was the pain of living that he no longer wanted to face. A life has been lost. Alan Bates had committed no crime. He was the victim, but we cannot punish these young boys as if they had pulled the trigger themselves. Their future is in your hands.

Judge Rinehart read the jury their instructions.

It was over. Janet did not care about the verdict. Dr. Smith and Ellen were there with her. Tom and Ellen drove her home to be with Christina. The jury would be deliberating for a while.

The boys went home with their parents to wait for the jury to reach a decision.

They got the call the next morning. The jury had made up their mind.

Both boys stood by their attorneys. The charges were read. The judge read the charges and then gave the slip to the bailiff.

"On the charge of causing bodily injury, we say not guilty. On the charge of malicious harassment, we say guilty."

The boys will be sentenced in 30 days.

Blake and Dwight expected a guilty verdict on the lesser charge. With faith, the boys would get probation. They would be with them until it was over.

About the Author

Ms. Milner was born in Ft. Riley Kansas. She is a Christian, mother, grandmother, author, and motivational speaker. Her mission is to give every child a voice. Claudette Milner is the author of the Children of Plains Estates series. The series includes:

Children of Plains Estates

Children of Plains Estates: Unheard Voices

Children of Plains Estates: Silent Tears.

Contact Us

Claudette.milner@gmail.com

www.claudettemilner.com

Claudette Milner

www.ingramcontent.com/pod-product-compliance
Lightning Source LLC
Chambersburg PA
CBHW071256130626
46556CB00003B/1344